Winner of the 28th Annual International 3-Day Novel Contest

Day Shift Werewolf

Jan Underwood

3-Day Books
Vancouver, Toronto

3-Day Books
341 Water Street, Suite 200
Vancouver, B.C., V6B 1B8
Canada

www.3daynovel.com

Printed and bound in Canada
Cover art ı Liz Trueblood
Design ı Jane Lightle, Bibelot Communications
Editor ı Jenn Farrell
Printer ı Hemlock Printers

Library and Archives Canada Cataloguing in Publication
Underwood, Jan, 1964-

Day Shift Werewolf
Jan Underwood

"Winner of the 28th Annual International 3-Day Novel Contest"

ISBN 1-55152-208-X
I. Title.
PS3621.N385D39 2006   813'.6   C2006-901098-6
Distributed in Canada by Jaguar
and in the United States by Consortium
through Arsenal Pulp Press

Acknowledgments

This book began as a mother-daughter bonding experience, and so I am indebted to my daughter, Majida, for inspiration and solidarity in the three-day-novel-writing process. Jenn Farrell, my editor, and Melissa Edwards and Barbara Zatyko of the 3-Day Novel Contest were a delight to work with. And I am most grateful to my parents, June and Jerry Underwood, who taught me much of what I know about reading and writing.

This one is for Majida.

Contents

honestly, I don't know what we're going to do with that boy. He won't be still for two minutes at a stretch. Always wandering off, sometimes at a critical moment. Take last night. We left the cabin together at dusk and herded through the woods. Andy was with us when we left. We were approaching a campground; there were, oh, four or five campers there, isolated; we would have gotten them all no problem. The campground was at the bottom of a little dale and we were just cresting the hill overlooking it when all of a sudden, it was, like, where the hell's Andy? We had to stop and go looking for him, all in a big noisy clump, trying not to draw attention to ourselves, because if we didn't get the campers, they might get us. We thrashed around in the woods half the night. Everyone was incensed. No; I was incensed; the others weren't, but they should have been. We finally found him back near the cabin, trying to climb a tree, if you can picture anything so ridiculous.

He doesn't grasp that we have to stick together. We're not fast. We're not strong. God knows we're not agile. Some of us aren't so bright. The only thing we've got going for us, really, is our ability to overwhelm people as a group. A kid all by himself like that? Well, assuming they knew not to touch him, they could catch him in a minute flat and take him away. Or kill him on the spot.

The thing is, Andy is one of the bright ones; he's always been a smart kid. I can't understand why he doesn't see the urgency here. Maybe he just doesn't want to. It makes me crazy.

So we're here in the cabin again, we haven't made any progress since the borough of Pleasant Grove about a week ago. It must have been a twenty-mile walk through the woods after that. Which is fine; none of us minds being in the woods—it's good cover—or walking forever. Except that it's a chore keeping Andy on track, moving forward nice and steady. But a week is a long time to go without human contact, and everybody starts to get itchy.

Personally, I think we should be grateful for small favours. I like staying in a cabin instead of milling around under the trees all day, because it makes it easier to corral Andy. Also, if it rains, we have shelter and don't have that annoying problem of our skin melting. To be honest I don't care about the pain—in reality it only stings—but the insult to my appearance is hard to take. That's been one of the most difficult things about all this for me, how ugly we've gotten. It rains, and your skin pocks when a raindrop hits, and it melts a little bit and kind of dribbles down your face. After three or four rainstorms we're a mess.

You know I'm not sure the others are as bothered as I am. They don't seem to care about anything any more, except for going out at night and getting people. Which is, now that I reflect on it, an appropriate attitude. Maybe I need to let go.

As I'm standing here thinking all this I realize Andy's not in the cabin. Shit! I should never have taken my eyes off him. I'm a bad mother. I just have this one job, it's the only thing I have to accomplish during the day, and I let it fall through the cracks. Now where is he?

I move to the door but there's Ron standing in front of it. Ron doesn't realize anything is wrong. He's taken his customary spot. To him one moment is no different than the next. He'll stand there all day and not budge an inch. A tornado could be happening outside and he'd just stand there patiently waiting for nightfall. Which is an admirable quality. Ron is steadfast. But right now we've got to find Andy, and Clueless here is making himself an obstacle. So I moan at him. Moan and then when that doesn't get his attention, I use my arm like a baseball bat and whack him on the shoulder.

Ron rotates toward me, slow and tilted like a gyroscope, and looks at me. His eyes are completely dead. There's no spark in there at all; I doubt he even remembers he's my husband. He turns, slow as molasses, to the window, to check the light. I can practically hear his brain labouring; he sees that it's not yet time to go out for the night. Then he gyrates in place, gazing around the room, and I know that he finally realizes: Andy is missing. So he kicks at the door until it opens and he shuffles out. The commotion attracts everyone's attention and everyone gets it. We have a pretty good herd instinct, I must say.

We all galumph out behind Ron and start looking for that darned kid.

"Andy!" we shout. Only it comes out "Mmmpphh!" because, of course, we've pretty much lost the ability to enunciate. "Andy!" People are moaning because the sunlight hurts. I don't know what it is with my son, whether the light doesn't hurt him as much, or whether he just doesn't care.

If we were still human we'd probably spread out and search in different directions. But of course we've got to stick together. So we plough forward in a big cumbersome bunch. I'm in the lead. I don't know whether they let me take the lead because I'm Andy's mom, or because I seem to be a little more inspired than a lot of them.

We don't want to go towards the clearing because then the sun will really get us. And we don't want to go towards the campground because we might be seen. So I take us in a southerly direction. I have no idea where my kid might be, so one way is as good as another. "Andy!"

He used to do this in the old days, too. I'd be in the kitchen and turn around and he'd be climbing the furniture, or darting out into the street to terrorize a neighbour's cat or something. You know what I think it is? I think he has ADHD. He's, like, bouncing off the walls all the time. Can't focus on one thing, ever; he's totally distractible. Has been his whole life.

The crazy thing is that he hasn't changed. I mean, the rest of us are pretty much transformed. And the hardest part is that, even more than back when we were human, he is making life so difficult. If there's one quality, one quality a zombie needs, it's focus. The single-minded drive to go out there and do your job, like a mail carrier: neither rain, nor hail, nor sleet, nor gloom of night, nor bullets from local police forces nor screaming crowds nor twenty-mile treks through the woods, shall stay these couriers from the faithful completion of their appointed rounds, which in our case is getting to the next batch of human beings and giving them a good squeeze and a little nibble. That's all we ever need to accomplish. It's very simple. And yet here's Andy zinging around, getting into everything, going places where he has no business, and completely ignoring his one duty.

Why couldn't he take after his father? Ron is a model zombie. Nothing distracts him. Nothing bothers him. Nothing deters him from his course. He doesn't speed up or slow down. He is as relentless, as reliable, as they come.

I'll tell you the truth, Ron was always a bit of a zombie. A man of monosyllables. A man of long periods of motionlessness, especially during the NFL playoffs. It's like he had an aptitude.

But Andy's not like his dad. He gets bored. Bored! That's his trouble. If you can imagine. The rest of us don't get bored. Zombies have no capacity to get bored. To them there is no past, no future, only the imperative to move forward together, nice and steady, and to infect the human beings in their path.

So we're thrashing around in the forest now, mmpphhing out Andy's name. We're not an athletic bunch and obstacles like fallen trees slow us down, because we can't go over them, we have to go around them, and sometimes it takes two or three tries. Then we're going down a slope, and this is dangerous because we don't have much of a capacity to slow ourselves down if we get going too fast; it's like rolling a log down a hill. You think you could do better? Try running cross-country without bending at the elbows or the knees. So pretty soon we're in a situation, we're all kind of scuffling down this hill and we're going too fast. I stop myself by deliberately running into a tree. But some of us get ahead of ourselves and two or three pitch face-forward into the earth and trip up the ones behind. God, what a mess. Now we're a big pile of felled zombies. I try to make my way down to where they are by moving from one tree to another, letting each tree stop me. Finally I get to the pile. Six or seven of us, just lying there with their arms out. Nobody is even moaning. I'd help them up but of course I can't bend at the waist. I don't know what the hell to do for them.

Those of us who haven't fallen are just standing around. No deep thinkers here. No creative minds. If they're not out infecting, they're pretty much worthless. Especially in the daylight. Daylight takes all the heart out of a zombie. In the daylight, a zombie just gives up on everything.

Looks like it's going to be up to me. Where is their group loyalty? Oh, I see how it is. Loyalty is their problem. They wouldn't abandon their clan. They'd stay here for the rest of eternity, give up on themselves, if it meant they could stick together. They'd all just stay right here, some standing, some fallen, until the Pleasant Grove Sheriff's Department eventually stumbled upon us and set fire to us. I do believe they wouldn't even resist. They'd all go down together, just for lack of a little ingenuity.

I think maybe I can use a fallen limb like a lever, push my comrades up to a position where the rest of us can reach their hands and pull them to standing. So I start looking around for a limb. It's got to be long enough to give me the power to lever up a 150-pound body, but light enough that I can nudge it over with my foot. What a job.

I start trudging around looking. My kinsmen, the ones still standing, begin to moan. I think they think I'm abandoning them. Well, there's no explaining. I won't go where they can't see me.

Just a little ways beyond the site of our disaster is a creek. I won't go in the creek, not if I don't want to melt like ice cream in July. But I can follow it downstream looking for limbs and that way I won't get lost. When I get there I hear splashing. My heart jumps. If it's campers, we're in trouble.

But it's not campers. It's Andy. Andy, whooping it up in the swimming hole, like no zombie you ever laid eyes on. I moan at him, as loud as I can, and he comes out of the water, obedient for once. His skin is dripping off him like chocolate sauce. He looks awful.

Andy follows me back to the prostrate zombies. I'm looking for good branches all the way back, but I don't see anything remotely usable. When we get to our clan members, Andy picks up the pace. He looks delighted. Well, as delighted as a zombie can look—there's not much we can do any more by way of facial expressions. It's more like a spark in his eye. He shuffles ahead of me, downright speedy, and then he bends at the waist!— and he pulls all the fallen ones up to standing, one after the other. I can hardly believe my eyes. So we all make our way, slow and stiff-legged, up the hill again, through the forest and to our old cabin. And I can't be mad at Andy for running off, because he's saved all our sorry zombie asses.

Back in the cabin now, I am shaken, and relieved. Are the others shaken? You'd think they would be, but they seem just the same as always. They live in the moment. Well, who knows what's going on with them internally? I suppose I look just like them. Stiff and dead-eyed. I hope to never see myself in a mirror again.

I'm beginning to think that Andy didn't get as badly infected as the rest of us. He's green enough, his skin looks just like ours. But that bending at the waist! Back when I was human, I had a touch of rheumatoid arthritis, and I'm telling you, I'd swap this zombie stiffness for arthritis any day. Arthritis is merely painful and incapacitating. You have no idea how uncomfortable and inconvenient it is to have no real use of your joints. And Andy's tolerance for the creek water! That's amazing. He's a good boy at heart. He did something important for his clan.

Still, I'm thinking that things can't go on like this. He helped us today, but half the time he's putting us at risk. He doesn't want to live the zombie life, I can see that. This hanging around in one spot all day and doing the same thing night after night is no life for him. He wants stimulation, he wants freedom. I see him gazing out the window. He doesn't have an appreciation for what we do. He lacks persistence. He lacks commitment. Beyond the woods, beyond Pleasant Grove, lies a whole world of other wonders that beckon to him. If he gets a chance, I can see he's going to make a break for it and not look back. I don't know what to do.

I guess I should stay in the present. That's really my job, after all. Focus, like a committed zombie, on the task at hand. The task at hand right now is to wait until nightfall, and then go out and get those campers if they're still there. The future will take care of itself.

The sun is lingering in the trees, and all is quiet, quiet. Ron is at the door and hasn't moved in three hours. Doesn't bother him one bit. An uncharitable thought runs through my mind: Ron's new zombie behaviour reminds me of nothing so much as his old bedroom behaviour. Clumsy, stiff-limbed, glassy-eyed, oblivious. The occasional inarticulate moan. I love my husband, but he always was useless in bed.

Everybody else is pretty much immobile, too. Just standing and staring into the middle distance. You wonder what zombies do during the day? I'll tell you: nothing. The sun hurts our eyes, you know, and makes us listless. Plus we can't risk getting caught. A good thing about these recent cuts to the National Park Service budget is how it's emptied out the forests. People don't want to come and camp where the outhouses don't get cleaned, they don't want to hike on unmaintained trails, and sometimes, like now, we luck out and find an old Park Service building no longer in use. So we have plenty of places to hide during the daylight hours. During the day, that's our one task: hide, stay quiet, stay out of the sun, do nothing. And at night, our one task is find people, and get 'em.

When the sun gets low enough, the clan starts to get itchy. We've been sub-dued all afternoon, but the desire to get out and infect starts to well up in us as the light dies. We get agitated. My kinsmen begin to rock back and forth and moan softly. I feel it, too. The drive is very strong. It gets uncomfortable waiting for the sun to set. We begin to shuffle together now, closing in near the door so we can burst out as soon as the sky is dark. Now the sun has set, but the paleness fades slowly. It is becoming almost unbearable. We are moan-ing loudly now, shifting weight from one flat foot to the other. Finally a few stars begin to appear, the eastern sky is a deepening blue. I think it's a few minutes too early still, but Ron can't stand it any more and kicks the door open, and we all surge out and begin the march towards the campground, and I'm glad, I don't care if we get caught, I love this pushing ahead and I don't have to take responsibility for making us all stay in that cabin one more minute when there are people to be infected and we're marching towards them, we're going to get them, we're going to get them soon. The earth underneath and the scrubby underbrush and the branches of trees and the leaves overhead all pass by as though I'm standing still and they're the ones that are moving. It feels effortless; I have no sensation. Everything has gone to black and white. I have eyes only for those campers. Here's the hill we've crested before, gently sloping down to the camping area. We spread out and go around a picnic table in two groups and come back together. There are their little tents, and now they've heard us and they're emerging, a man, a woman, three more people behind, their little beams of flashlights are making tunnels of yellow in the dark, I hear their screaming now, but it sounds faraway and tinny, like on an old radio with poor reception, we've made a circle around them now and are closing in, the desire to get them is overwhelming, I see limbs thrashing, the yellow tunnels are streaking up and down, we squeeze in until the arms of the clan are all around the campers, all our collective arms, chests, ploughing in and squeezing until we've got them in a big relentless inescapable zombie hug.

The yellow tunnels of flashlight are lying on the ground now. All is quiet, quiet.

We can relax. We feel the satisfaction of a good night, a job well done. The new zombies will lie on the ground for a few hours while the infection courses through them, and before daybreak they will join our clan, and we'll be five stronger. Since I've been in the clan we've taken on both Pleasant Grove and this campground, building our group up to about sixteen. The next town over is Stevens' Ferry. It's a bigger town than Pleasant Grove, which of course means greater danger, but also greater potential.

Is Andy still with us? My heart jumps. I'd forgotten all about him in my single-minded drive to get the campers. I turn. There he is. He's poking at a tent with a stick. Now he's playing with the zipper. Where is his sense of pride? I wonder if Ron is ashamed to have such a son. But I look over at Ron and he is as expressionless as a tree. Calm, having accomplished his mission. But without emotion.

There's no sense going back to the cabin; from here we'll move forward towards Stevens' Ferry. When the new zombies awaken and rise, we shuffle away from the campsite, cross a Forest Service road, find a copse where we can stay.

Daybreak. We crouch under a thicket of blackberries. The new zombies are more human than we are—more limber, and more frightened. They'll get used to it. They'll stiffen up, and flatten out, over the next few days. Andy picks blackberries and hums. He is the only one of us who hums. It's annoying to listen to. He pokes an anthill with a stick. He makes mud pies of dirt and spit. He somersaults, alarming the other zombies, who have to shuffle out of his way so they don't get knocked over. He tries to climb the blackberry bush, scratches up his hands on the thorns, and cries. He's the only one of us who cries, too. His tears melt two long tracks down his cheeks, leaving long skinny troughs in his face.

Nightfall. We trek through the forest. Of course we don't have a map. And nobody could read one if we did. We hone in on campsites and townships with a kind of internal radar. I know we're not choosing the most efficient route to Stevens' Ferry. We just have to do the best we can, coming to obstacles, going around them, ponderous. I guess it doesn't matter. It shouldn't matter, anyway. There is no tomorrow. There is only the task at hand.

Daybreak. We stop in a grove of trees. This isn't as good as a cabin or a blackberry thicket, because we're not completely protected from the light. It's uncomfortable. Our skin burns, our eyes burn. We fall limp, passive. Each of us stands as close to a tree as we can get, leaning our heads against the bark. Andy spends the morning repeatedly jumping up and trying to pull my hair. He can really jump, that kid, he can bend at the knees, and if I had any energy I'd whack him with my arm like a baseball bat, but under this sun I just can't. I used to have really nice hair. Now there's not much of it left, and Andy is pulling out what remains, handful after handful. I moan and stomp in place, but it doesn't make any difference.

Nightfall. We trod, we trod. Andy sees a raccoon and chases after it, and we waste hours corralling him back.

Daybreak. Another grove of trees. I am growing weary. It's always the same, and it's always uncomfortable. The only satisfaction is in infecting, and that doesn't happen very often.

Nightfall. At last Stevens' Ferry is in view, a spread of twinkling lights like bright seeds scattered over the dark landscape. If we were human, this is the moment when we would gather and make a plan. But we can't make a plan; we can't communicate. Each of us has to take it on faith that the others have the same goal in mind, that we'll stick together, that we'll focus in on one group of people to infect, that we'll be mindful of the possibilities of getting caught, that we won't fail to leave ourselves an opening. I like to think that all this understanding comes with the infection, that it is part of the zombie instinct. But I'm not completely convinced that it works this way. I think maybe up to now we've just been lucky. I think maybe some of my clansmen don't know what they're doing. Even my Ron. Disloyal as it is to say so.

Now that the town is in view, everyone is getting worked up. It's late, it must be three or four in the morning. Personally I think we should hold back another day. With only a couple of hours to go until sunrise, there's a good chance we won't be able to hit the town and retreat again safely. But there's no stopping the clan. They're beginning to bob and groan. They're beginning to speed up. I just hope they don't take the slope too fast; I doubt they learned their lesson back near the creek.

Andy is alongside me, picking up stones in the road and chucking them at trees. He can bend at the elbows. Now he's chucking stones at signposts: we're starting to come to "Steven's Ferry, one mile," and "Steven's Ferry, next two exits." In their excitement my kinsmen plough right over some of these signs. "Highway 6" goes down in a crumple. "Downtown Stevens' Ferry, Exit 4" is knocked to one side. We zombies are filling the whole width of the exit ramp, ploughing towards the city centre. There's not much activity at this time of night. One lone guy is stumbling up the road—like he's just come out of a bar— and we swarm around him and squeeze him and gobble up his brain before he knows we're coming. A couple of teenagers in the back seat of a car hear the commotion and don't have the sense to keep their heads down. We see their curious white faces in the window and in a moment's time we've surrounded the car and started to rock it back and forth. The clan is in a frenzy. We've got those kids good. They'll never get out. We will rock that car until we shake them unconscious, or we'll stay there, single-minded, until they starve to death. But we don't have to do either of those things, because the boy, in a fit of teenage bravado, takes what he thinks is an opportunity to throw the car door open and jump out, wielding a jack. We aren't strong, but he doesn't know how little we care if we get hit with metal objects. In about ten seconds we've got him. And the girl just gives herself up without a fight.

We leave them, the teenagers and the drunk, in the street. They'll catch up to us after the infection has set in. We've got more work to do, because in a town this size, the possibilities are endless. We're elated, as elated as zombies can be. "Welcome to Steven's Ferry, Population 106,343" is trampled underfoot. "Stevens' Ferry Chamber of Commerce, next left" as well. We pass some shops, a corner grocery, and a café, all closed up for the night of course, and come upon a nightclub. Oh, a nightclub is an excellent opportunity. All those people conveniently packed in tight. The bouncer is ours before he has time to demand our IDs. We stumble inside, under painfully flashing lights and thunderous music, and double our numbers before the first song is over. My clansmen are greedy and I can see they want to keep going, but when we move out of the club again the eastern sky is rimmed in white. They don't seem to notice, and begin to shuffle on down the street towards the Chamber of Commerce. If there are human beings within reach, a zombie is going to go after them, even if he's cutting his own throat to do so. I can see that focus is not always in our best interests.

I moan to get their attention and head back to the highway. After a half a block I turn in place to see if they've had the sense to follow, but they haven't, the morons. They're lurching down Main Street with their arms stuck straight out in front of them like they've all just been sent over from central casting. The drunk and the teenagers have joined them. Amazing how quickly the infection knocks out all ability to think for oneself. They're just a big dumb herd. And they're going to march straight into the nets of the police without thinking twice about it. Look, I get as much satisfaction out of infecting as the next zombie, but I know when to quit, for Christ's sake. I don't have a death wish. These guys, they just seemed to stop caring.

Now where's my son? He's not with them. I rotate in place. Andy is on the roof of the bar, up the road. Looks like he shimmied up the rainspout, God knows how. He's waving to get my attention. When he sees that he's got it, he points. Good boy! He's communicating! Pointing is something any zombie could do, but I've never seen any of us try it. Down here on the ground I can't see what he's pointing at, but I don't need to, because soon enough, I hear it: police sirens, and the squeal of tires. Over a couple blocks where the clan is, police cars are converging. I'm rooted to my spot for a minute, thinking. Then Andy is beside me. He grabs my hand, and together we shuffle up the exit ramp as fast as we can manage. Behind us in the distance I can hear the moaning and the shambling of flat feet, and engines roaring. We cross the highway and duck into the woods. Here comes the clan now, returning just the way we came. It never occurs to them to split up, to create a diversion, to find a better hiding place than the open stands of trees where we've spent the last day. Or to stay and squeeze and chew on the police officers; that would be their best tactic, right there. But they've gone into flight mode now, and they'll keep running until they run over a cliff or into the ocean. Here they come, barrelling back over the highway with the police right behind them. The zombies are probably following us, because somehow they've come to think of us as leaders. If it were nighttime, I'd charge out there and try to get us all to surround the police cars. Bullets and nightsticks of course have no deterrent effect on us. We'd be able to out-squeeze a small police force pretty handily, I think. But the sun has now come up in earnest; the highway is bathed in yellow light, and I think we would lack the moral force to see the job through to the end. In the light, everyone will just go limp and passive. The cops could round us up with their nightsticks, snap leg irons on us, and we'd go along to the jailhouse as cooperatively as cows. Assuming that these officers of the law know what we are. If they touched us, of course, they'd get the infection. Not as quickly as if we closed in on them and diseased them deliberately, but sooner or later. That fact makes the panic of my fellows even more ridiculous. Why are they running away? Morons!

I am faced with a decision. My duty as a zombie, and my strong desire in spite of my better judgment just now, is to stay with my clan to the bitter end. I could rush out there and try to save them, or join them, or stand here waving and let them join me, and we could all rally together or perish together trying.

But I can also see that with a tiny effort I can escape them, and escape the cops, too. Andy and I can slip into the woods unseen and save our own skins. And don't I owe him loyalty too, my one and only son?

There's my Ron, hobbling lock-kneed over the road as persistently as he can. He moves like a zombie now but he's still got that paunch from his football-viewing days. It hurts my heart to see him. We belong together. He's my husband. This group of zombies is my family. What use are we alone? We have to stick together, that's the zombie imperative.

I've made up my mind. I take my boy by the hand and march, with determination, with focus, to my tribesmen. They are moaning, coming over the highway into the woods. Police cars follow, pull to a stop sideways in the road, and officers tumble out. They are shouting, they are pointing their pistols at us. It doesn't matter. We are together. My clansmen swarm up about me and into the woods we plunge. I don't know where we're going. I do know that we are untiring. Humans will eventually give in to exhaustion, but we can keep going forever. I don't have to worry about cliffs and oceans. There are no cliffs or oceans here, none for so far into the future that I don't have to think about it. There is no future. There is only now, and this ploughing, with my own folk. Impervious to the bullets now ringing, faraway and tinny. Impervious to the scratches of branches and thorns. I still have Andy by the hand. We are in the forest, and everything has gone to black and white. I don't hear the police any more, or see them. They've fanned out, I guess, they've gone elsewhere. Then suddenly they've surrounded us. I am not worried. We can dispense with them in a matter of minutes, if we pull together.

But from the first whiff of that terrible smell, from the first flare-up before my eyes, I know they're onto us. They know what we are, and they know what to do to us. The smell of wood smoke, and then flames, flames ahead of me, flames to my left, to my right, they've made a circle of fire and trapped us inside, and we are doomed. I swivel, looking for an out. My tribesmen are not looking. They are panicking. They are rocking back and forth, lowing like cattle. Andy grabs my hand. The flames are growing fast. In this late summer dryness, the forest grass and low brush catches like paper and crackles as it burns. Smoke is beginning to drift into the circle. Ron is blank-faced, dead-eyed, rocking. The flames are growing into a wall, impenetrable, head-high. The only place in the circle not yet ablaze is a spot where a sign for the National Forest stands. Flames are licking its thin wooden legs. Andy, my jumper, is there is a split second. He jumps right up onto it. He turns, bends at the waist, and hoists me up. We both pitch over the other side of the sign. Andy pulls me to standing.

We should run. Andy is tugging at my arm. But our family is going to be burnt to the ground. I can't leave them. I swing my arm like a baseball bat at the National Park sign. This is pointless; I'm not strong. I kick at the sign's thin legs. Andy kicks, too. Our feet are getting burnt. The legs of the sign, which are quickly becoming charcoal, crumble and the sign buckles and goes down. I moan at my kinsmen, and they see, and they come. They come in a stampede, and the police are powerless to stop them.

Afternoon. Back in the blackberry bushes. We have only lost two to the humans. The Stevens' Ferry police force is, for the moment, stalled. For the moment, we are safe.

I have been rattled all afternoon. My mind is racing. I look at my kinsmen. Are they rattled? They stand in the bushes, staring into the middle distance. Their eyes are dead. It is as though nothing has happened. I wonder if they even remember. I wonder if they realize that the law is on our trail, that we were nearly all wiped out, that we are in mortal danger, that we will have to be exquisitely vigilant from now on.

I don't think they have it in them to be vigilant.

If I could, I'd twiddle my thumbs. But of course I have a very limited range of thumb motion. I'll tell you the truth, I'm sick of this. This zombie life is no life. When it's uneventful, it's downright dull. And when it's eventful, it's dangerous. And I can see that my clansmen are not going to be of any use. Andy and I risked our necks to save the rest of them. Would they do the same for us?

Dusk. The zombies are getting agitated. Ron is standing at the den-like entrance to the blackberry thicket where we entered, rocking back and forth. I can feel it in my own chest, too. Itchy. We are within reach of human beings. I can see what's happening: they want to go out infecting. I want to shout, are you kidding me? After what happened today? But there's no reasoning with them, even if I could speak. They are starting to moan. And I think: this zombie life is bullshit. I look over at Andy. He's pulling leaves off the bushes, tearing them into confetti, and showering himself with them. This is no life for my only son. He needs stimulation. He needs freedom. And it occurs to me that I am more like my son than I realized.

I take Andy's hand, and I look into his eyes. There is a spark there. Without moaning to the others, I pull him through the opening of the blackberry thicket. Beyond the woods, beyond Pleasant Grove, the wide world is visible, and we are going there together. We make a break for it, and we don't look back.

Part 2
Day Shift Werewolf

I know this: it's me they're talking about. Jack and Lobo, at the water cooler. I've just come into the foyer, taking off my jacket, when I hear them.

"You know they're gonna put him on the day shift," Lobo says.

"The day shift! Why?"

"The guy hasn't made quota in six months, man. And you know who has to make up the difference. You and me, buddy, that's who."

"They're firing him?"

"Not technically. I mean, the guy's gotta eat, right? But, basically, yeah. And good riddance. He's dead weight."

I'm torn between crouching here so I can hear what else they have to say about me, and charging around the corner to put them to shame. But then Lon, my boss, appears in the foyer and says, "Warren, can I see you for a minute?"

Casual as pie, I say, "Sure," and like I'm not worried about a thing I check my mailbox—like I ever get any mail—right in front of Jack and Lobo, before I stroll into Lon's office.

It's an act, though, and we all know it, because I'm getting the boot.

They can't actually fire me. Union rules. But getting put on the day shift is tantamount to getting fired, because how is a werewolf supposed to do his job in the daytime? Granted, the moon is sometimes visible during the day, and that's what Lon tells me. He says they're not suspending my license; I can still catch what I need for my own consumption and collect a commission on whatever I bring in over that amount. But the fact that they're doing this means they expect very little of me. I won't even have to clock in any more. They don't even expect me to show up for work, period.

"I see," I tell Lon, in an unconcerned voice, like he's just told me we're changing the office colour scheme. "All righty then. Thanks for filling me in." I shake his hand and stroll out. As I'm leaving I see the secretary scraping my name off my mailbox.

Son of a bitch. How did it come to this?

The quotas have been going up every year, for one thing. Time was when most of us made a decent living by putting in a reasonable number of hours, you know? Guys like Lobo and Jack, they were table setters. And I was one of them. A little on the low side in terms of the numbers I brought in, but nothing to be ashamed of. And the work environment was supportive; it was comradely. It wasn't this cutthroat competition. But then they started bringing in these big beefy guys, guys like Harry, guys like Major. Sluggers who drove the quotas through the roof. Guys that made the rest of us have to run ourselves ragged trying to keep up. Some of these wolves are Type A, driven, ambitious businessmen who want to get rich. And they do. They'll do their wolfing at, say, a rock concert, where they get twenty or thirty bodies a night. Those guys make a killing. Others make quota in two or three nights and then spend the rest of the month in Atlantic City, or Miami, living the easy life. A guy like me just can't do that. For one thing, I don't have the stamina. Plus, crowds make me feel queasy. I do things the old-fashioned way: one, two bodies a night, working steady, not taking a lot of nights off. Respectable. Loyal. Dependable. I guess loyalty and dependability don't count for anything any more. I guess sixteen years with the same company doesn't matter any more, either. It's all about the body count, and if you're not a top dog, you're out.

Aw, hell. What am I going to do with myself? I'm gonna have to get another job is what I'm gonna have to do. I won't kid myself, I can't live off the commissions from the bodies I can bring in. Without my salary I'll have to find something else. Like what? This is what I was born to do. This is what my family has done for generations. It's a good thing Pop didn't live to see me get fired. The shame would have killed him.

It's not like Stevens' Ferry is teeming with job opportunities, either. I could move to a bigger city. But I like it here. It's quiet, it's quaint, and it's surrounded by forest, which is a good place to wolf up.

I spend the night moping.

In the morning I decide to go see Molly. She's not a girlfriend or anything like that. She just cuts my hair. And gives me good advice. Except I haven't seen her in a while, because the last time I went in there, she made me mad.

"Not too short in the back," I told her. "I don't like it too short."

"It looks bad, Warren."

"Leave it."

"It looks bad long. Let me cut it."

"I like my mullet," I growled.

"It looks bad."

"Just do what I'm paying you for," I said, and we didn't talk for the rest of the haircut.

So I haven't seen her in a while. But she's a friend, and I could use one right now, so I walk down past the Chamber of Commerce and over to Molly's salon. Her sign is on the door, Be back at___, and the little cardboard clock reads eleven a.m. Darn it. Guess I'll go find a newspaper and take a look at the want ads. I tramp along Main, past Tempest in a Teacup, which is a café, past the courthouse. Past the new downtown renovation banners that read, Steven's Ferry Welcomes You! Past Stevens Ferry Fries, which is a burger joint. Now here's something that raises my hackles: public misspellings. Living where I do I see it every day. Our town wasn't founded by some dude named Steve, he didn't run "Steven's ferry." It was somebody Stevens. You know, like, Mr. Aloysius Stevens. I know this: it's not Steven's Ferry, it's Stevens' Ferry. With the apostrophe after the "s". Except people nowadays don't know where to put apostrophes, so they just toss them in anywhere. Or, like the folks at Stevens Ferry Fries, they throw up their hands and surrender; they just leave out the apostrophe altogether. And what bristles my fur most is that the government does it. Our elected officials can't punctuate their own city name properly. It's spelled multiple ways on city signs, for crying out loud.

Here's a newspaper box. I find a quarter in my jeans pocket, buy a paper, and tuck it under my arm for later. Five minutes to ten. Too early to go back to Molly's. I walk on past the department stores, the pharmacy, cross the bridge over the river, and pace around the grounds of the museum for a little while. Avoiding the want ads as long as I can. Finally I plop down on a bench and open up the paper. First I check the weather page. Full moon tonight. Great. The universe is thumbing its nose at me.

Let me set the record straight: that whole thing about werewolves only being able to transform under a full moon is bunk. Of course the full moon is a Power Night. But any of us worth his or her incisors should be able to wolf up on any night when the moon is visible. Half-moon, waxing and waning gibbous, even crescent. The only nights that aren't good for wolfing are new moon nights and times when it's really cloudy. That's when we usually take a night or two off. But listen to me, talking like I'm still employed. Why should I even give a damn now? I mean, they obviously don't give a damn about me. I'm not going to work like a dog just because it's a Power Night, and go crawling back to them with a bunch of bodies. I'm gonna find another job.

Yeah, doing what? I turn to the want ads. They go on for pages. This is so overwhelming. Maybe Molly'll have some ideas. I leave the newspaper on the bench and start back towards Main Street, hands in my pockets.

Oh, Jesus, a dog. Thing is, humans don't usually know about me. They just think I'm an ugly guy, a guy who was born with the hairy back gene. But dogs, man. Dogs always know. And this one is no happy-go-lucky Lab, either. She's a massive hulk of a German shepherd and already, from half a block away, her great black ears and tail are up and she's staring right at me. I do the omega dog thing, eyes down, tailbone tucked. Deferential. A nobody, a nobody who, I promise you, ma'am, knows his place. The German shepherd is having none of it. She lets out a long low growl like a prelude to murder. If I looked up right now I'd see her teeth bared at me. I turn tail and run as hard as I can. She's after me like a shot. I hear her four paws galloping, I hear her breath behind me. At the end of this block is an annex to the museum. I cut through the grass and make for its entrance. Slam down on the bar that pushes the door open. I'm in an empty hallway. There's no exhibit going on in the annex right now, I guess. I put my hands on my knees to catch my breath. The door to the annex is pneumatic; it closes by itself, slowly. Here comes the shepherd, just swift enough to slip through before the door shuts. Now we're in the hallway together. She's growling like an engine. I back away slowly, slowly, head down, to the far end of the hall. There's another door there. Please God may it not be locked. I reach behind me, feel for the doorknob, turn it. It's open. Dash through, slam it shut. The shepherd hurls herself against the other side of the door and snarls in rage. Oh, man, that was close.

So I'm in a stairwell that leads to the basement of the museum, which I follow down into the bowels of the building. I have to stay down there a while and try to recover my dignity. For the second time today I'm thinking about my Pop, and how appalled he would be to know what kind of werewolf he had for a son. Afraid of dogs. That's some werewolf. I dwell there in the semi-dark until I can't stand my own company any more. Then I find an exit, and go on over to Molly's.

Which is a little awkward in itself. I'm wondering if we're going to need to talk about the last time I got my hair cut. When I've worked up the courage to make an apology, I push open the door to the salon, casual as pie. To my surprise, Molly's all warm and happy to see me, and kind of sad at the same time, and I realize that word's already gotten out about my job. It's a safe bet I'm not in the doghouse over the mullet any more. "Hey," I say.

"Hey," she says.

I sit in her plushy leather barber chair. I don't need a haircut, but I like this plushy chair.

"I heard," she says.

"Yeah."

Molly comes over and sits in the barber chair next to mine. It's pumped up high, ready for action, and her feet dangle.

"It really bites."

"Yeah," I concur.

Molly waggles her dangling feet. "So what are you gonna do?"

"What would you do if you were me, Mol?" I ask. "I mean, I guess I need a new job. I'm kind of stumped."

Molly holds her chin in her hand, thinking. "You know?" she says. "This could be a real opportunity for you to find yourself. Find a true vocation. You know, a calling."

A calling. My parents were werewolves, and their parents before them. I thought we were all called to be Followers of The Moon. I was never raised to think of anything else. To do something else goes against my upbringing, my heritage, my blood. It's a shame to my family name. A true vocation? What am I, if not a werewolf? What other passions, what other skills, could I possibly possess? "Jesus, Molly," I say.

"Come on," she says, her eyes brightening. She leans forward in her high barber chair, the points of her shoes coming to rest, a little pigeon-toed, on the footrest. She looks cute. "What do you like to do? What do you dream about? If you could do anything at all."

"Aw, Jeez." I scratch the hairy back of my neck. "I dunno."

"What do you do when you're not working? You garden, right?"

"Yeah." Pretty proud of my beefsteak tomatoes, actually.

"Okay. This is just a brainstorm. What else? You read the motorcycle magazines when you come in here."

"Yeah." I don't actually have a motorcycle. I've thought about saving for one.

"You could open a Harley shop here in Stevens' Ferry," Molly says.

We go on in this vein for a while. I can't say I actually have any brilliant ideas about my calling when I leave, but I feel better. It cheered me up to see that Molly cared, that she made an effort to help me out. That she was so, well, sparky in my presence.

Warren, don't kid yourself, I mutter. A woman like Molly would never be interested in a guy like you. A no-talent, hairy-back guy with a bad haircut. An unemployed hairy-back guy. Put it out of your mind.

So my good mood doesn't last very long. And I find I'm overcome with sleepiness. Day shift, huh? After a lifetime of nocturnal habits, this is going to take some getting used to. Forget the brainstorming. I'm going home to take a nap.

It's evening when I wake. I know this: whatever new job I take, it's going to have to have flexible hours. There is just no way I can go diurnal.

I'm hungry, and not really in the mood for leftovers. There's nothing in the fridge but an old arm and a jar of pickles. I don't even know if that arm's still good. I grab it and give it a sniff. Ugh—too far gone. I wrap it in plastic and take it to the outside trashcan.

The moon is up and it's a beauty, glowing yellow and perfectly round, hovering near the horizon. No reason I couldn't go hunting for myself tonight. It is a Power Night, after all.

So I take a little stroll around town to see what's what. A couple doors down they're having a party, but I'm not going to eat my neighbours. That's another thing about Stevens' Ferry: the possibilities for slaughter are limited. It's kind of an unspoken agreement that we don't hunt the locals. Those heavy hitters at the company, a lot of them travel to Seattle or Tacoma to keep their numbers up. But I don't like to drive. I prefer to get around on foot or on public transportation and prey on visitors and tourists. It does mean slimmer pickings, though.

Downtown, at the convention centre, there's a gathering of Young Republicans. That sounds pretty palatable. I find a doorway facing away from the main boulevard and wolf up. Then I go into the centre from the back and prowl around for a while. On the fifth floor I find a sauna. It's so steamy inside I can hardly see a thing, but it looks like there's just one guy here, a gauzy brown shape in the haze. Perfect. I slip in, slit his throat with a steady claw and have a Young Republican for dinner.

Here's a revelation. This man should have been a delicacy. His flesh is tender. He's been well fed. His blood is iron-rich. He's clean and lightly steamed from
22

sitting in the sauna. Yet I find I don't like him very much; I mean, I don't like the way he tastes. And I realize, now that I've thrown open the doors of self-examination, that deep down I've never really cared for man-flesh. I always told myself I just had a small appetite, but now that I reflect on it, I never get tired of my tomatoes and zucchinis. I know this, with sudden and terrible knowing: it's human meat that I don't love.

I feel deeply, deeply subversive. So stunned am I by this new knowledge that I forget to leave the scene of the crime in any timely fashion, but sit there in the steam and blood, pondering my destiny. I come from a very long line of meat and potato men. Pop would roll over in his casket if he knew.

Of course, Pop did die of coronary artery disease. Like most of my family. No silver bullets for them. Not many of us have the honour of martyrdom, you understand. Mostly it's heart attacks, strokes, atherosclerosis.

My fur is soaking wet and I'm too warm. I'd better get out of here.

Back at home, still feeling dizzy, I look at myself in the mirror. I say to myself, "Who are you, Warren? Who are you, really?" I get a crazy urge to shave and I do it.

Morning is upon me and I should get some sleep. But I can't. I lie on my mattress all morning and think about my calling. What can I possibly be meant to do? I wasn't kidding when I said I had no skills. A motorcycle shop? I don't know the first thing about running a business. And to tell the truth, I don't want to work in retail. I'm not good with people. I only want to eat them. No! I don't even want to eat them any more. I want work that I can do on my own.

I'm not good with my hands. Well, except for clawing people's organs out, but that's hardly surgery. I guess I have a steady enough hand.

Still, I don't know how to repair anything. I can spell, but nobody's going to pay me to do that.

At one in the afternoon I've had it with insomnia and I decide to get up and clean out my closets. I pull everything out and chuck it all in the living room: toilet paper, flowered bed sheets, a bottle of bloodstain remover, vacuum cleaner bags, sewing kit, extra-strength dental floss, extra-strength mouthwash, clothespins, a hacksaw, photo albums, dog food for slow nights, an extra set of curtains. I make a heap in the living room and I take the old living room curtains down, too, intending to put up the other set instead. But suddenly I'm dog-tired, and I lose heart for sorting that big pile of crap. The pile reminds me somehow of the need to find my calling. Both seem insurmountable. I don't know where to begin.

No. I do know where to begin. I should just scrap it all. Scrap my whole life, my whole existence, and start over somewhere else. Move to the big city. Change my name. Make new friends. Leave wolfing, leave Stevens' Ferry behind me altogether. Go back to school. Start a new career. Start a new life. That's what I should do. That's what I'm going to do.

In a grand symbolic gesture I gather up an armload of crap from the living room floor, take it outside, and dump it in the outside garbage can on top of the old rotting arm. Three, four armloads later, my garbage cans are full, my closets are empty, and I'm on my way to wiping the slate of my selfhood clean so I can rewrite myself.

I go to use the bathroom, find there's no toilet paper, shuffle over to the linen closet in the hall with my pants around my ankles, realize the extra toilet paper is in the heap in the living room, shuffle out there, realize the extra toilet paper is now in the garbage can with all the other useful and useless items of my former life. Then the doorbell rings. And Molly peeks in the living-room window, now free and clear of curtains, to see if I'm home.

If I had a pistol and a silver bullet, I'd martyr myself right now.

The alternative is to retreat, pull up my pants, and answer the door casual as pie. "Hi!" Molly says. She seems as sparky as yesterday. Maybe she didn't see me. "I just came by to see how you're doing."

"I'm doing okay," I tell her.

"Wanna go for a walk?" she says.

So we do. In the late afternoon sunshine, we stroll through my tree-lined neighbourhood and shoot the breeze. I'm relieved to get to think about something besides my job for a while. Molly is chatty and relaxed.

Then she asks the question I dread. "Have you thought some more about your career situation?" she says.

I'm going to tell her the decision I've reached. Funny how, even though I'm doing the right thing, I don't relish letting her know I'm leaving.

But I don't get to answer her, because when we reach Main Street we see some commotion. "Wonder what's up," she says.

Something is awry here. A bunch of signposts have been knocked down. All the grass in the lawns and parking strips of this section of Main has been trampled, like a herd of cattle passed over it.

Some of our fellow townspeople are out surveying the damage. Harry, one of my former colleagues, is standing in the street, shaking his head. "Vandals," he says when he sees Molly and me. "Dog-gonedest thing. They pushed over a whole bunch of signs and damaged a car. Tore the place up good."

Somebody else chimes in. "They wrecked the dance floor over at the disco and scared off a bunch of people. Some of the folks who were out dancing took off and haven't come back home, I heard."

"The city's on it," a third person says. "I heard they've already made a bunch of arrests. The police were out at six o'clock this morning. And the mayor's already getting a crew together to make repairs."

Main Street looks like hell. Some of the new downtown renovation banners are lying in the street, muddied. Parking meters have been bent. There's even a telephone pole askew.

"I need to check on my salon," Molly says. We head straight there. Her place is untouched. But Stevens Ferry Fries has a broken window. The misspelled "Steven's Ferry Museum, next right" sign is lying in the street.

"Who would do this?" I say. "And why?"

Molly and I part ways. I head back home, slowly, looking over the damage as I go. I find I'm really broken up about this. Surprising how hard it hits me. Mayor Bajolaluna is actually a cousin of mine; I think I'll call her up and see if she could use my help on the cleanup crew.

I realize that I really love this town. Stevens' Ferry is home. I grew up here. I belong here. I don't know what I'm going to do about my calling. But I know this: I can't leave.

A few days later I seek Molly out again. I find I'm eager to see her and get her perspective. We go for another walk, this time along the river.

"How's the job hunt going?" she asks.

I find myself spilling out my innermost feelings to her. That I feel under a lot of pressure to come up with my calling. That I'm lost. That I'm overwhelmed.

"You know," Molly says. "You don't have to figure it out all at once. This might be a good time to just explore. Maybe take a class, or shadow some people in different jobs."

"You think?"

"Sure. You can't find yourself all at once. It's a process. And meanwhile, you know, you can find some small jobs just to get by."

"Yeah," I tell her, warming to the idea, "like the cleanup crew. I called my cousin to volunteer, and she said there might even be some paid work, and I should swing by City Hall and check it out."

"Let's go right now," Molly says, smiling at me.

I'm encouraged. I sure like Molly's company, too. So maybe I don't have to change everything all at once. Maybe small steps are okay. "You know what?" I say. It feels safe to try out new ideas with Molly. "I'm thinking of giving up red meat."

"Interesting," she tells me.

We cross the bridge and amble into lovely downtown Stevens' Ferry. Things here are getting straightened up, the parking meters replaced, the trampled grass replanted. Molly slips her hand into mine.

We steer over to City Hall. And right there in the front window is a help-wanted ad. Sign Painter, it reads. Steady hand needed for stencilling. They must want somebody to replace the signs that got knocked over during the vandalism. And I realize: this is my chance to rectify the city's improper punctuation.

It may not be a calling. But it is an opportunity. The universe is giving me the thumbs-up. "This is my new job!" I tell Molly, excited. "This job is meant for me!"

"Go on," my new girlfriend tells me. "Go inside and apply right now."

I know this: I am a lucky dog.

Part 3
Devil in Pink

I am the evil twin.

That's the short version. The truth is a little more complicated. Let me explain it to you.

I am commissioned to travel to earth and inhabit the body of a little girl. Her name is Sara. As far as Sara is concerned, she is one of a pair of twins. She does not remember ever having been without me. We are identical. We are inseparable. A pair of little darlings with ringlets of angelic hair and enormous blue eyes.

Sara's experience is that she is a well-behaved little girl, and that I am the naughty one. I am the one who breaks windows, steals dollies, throws peas on the floor and smears my poop on the wall. Sara stands by and looks aghast. She tries to talk me out of my crimes. She tattles on me.

But of course the reality is that I live in Sara's mind. As far as her parents are concerned, Sara is this complicated little being: an angel one day, a devil the next. It's Sara doing it all, the good and the ugly. And soon we'll be coming up to the truly interesting part, because Sara is getting older now, and starting to talk about her twin, and her parents are beginning to think that she is not only moody and unpredictable but loony as a bird.

Nobody, of course, is ever going to figure out that Sara is neither crazy nor a twin, but that Beelzebub has assigned a minor demon to craft a little mini-Hades of their lives.

I'll tell you what I like about my job. I have a lot of creative freedom. I am at liberty to design my own trouble, to enact any evil I can invent, within certain limits, of course. I can't have a three-year-old start a nuclear war, but I can probably orchestrate her parents' divorce, for instance. That's rewarding.

There's another bonus to this particular assignment I hadn't foreseen, which is that I find I rather enjoy being a child. For example, I gave Sara colic as a baby. Even through all the screaming and thrashing around, I have to admit it was pretty swell to be held and coddled and fed warm milk in a bottle. The toddler years were fun, too. Opportunities to exercise my skills—throwing tantrums, screaming "No!"—were plentiful, and as a perk I got to be carried all the time. Dark angels, you see, don't get to have these experiences, even when they are very new.

This is by far the longest I've been on one assignment. In college I learned to send the common cold around and write computer viruses. For my honours project I figured out how to make sure socks never come out of the dryer with their mates. All those socks? They're collected together in one room, piled up in one gigantic sock mountain. Some small-time crooks, when they get sent to Hell, have to spend eternity matching socks from that giant pile.

After I graduated I started out making weather annoyances, like humidity and inconvenient rainstorms. (I've ruined six outdoor weddings.) When I'd proven my mettle on little evils, they let me have more challenging work. One great thing about being a demon is I get to travel a lot, geographically and in time, too. I took part in the Crusades and in several wars. Just in minor ways, of course: gangrening people's feet, jamming people's rifles. Wars, now there's a niche. A demon who gets licensed in wars will never be out of work. But I'm more interested in interpersonal miscommunication. I started taking on jobs where I could stir up trouble between individuals. Doppelganging looked like an interesting opportunity, because I had never messed with a family before.

And family life turns out to suit me. It's full, if I dare say it, of sparkle and enchantment.

Take our room. It's done in shades of pink, with a theme of winged horses. We have Pegasus headboards on our beds (really just the one bed, but Sara looks around our room and sees two of everything), Pegasus lamps, Pegasus bedspreads. We've amassed a huge collection of plastic horses. I do love those horses. We play horses every day. We also have swimming lessons and bell choir. Wednesdays we have playgroup, where they give us animal crackers and we dig in the sandbox. I'm telling you, these are benefits I never imagined when I signed on for this job. Demons don't have childhoods, after all. We miss out on all these experiences that really develop a sense of wonder and magic in a person.

Sara and I are going to be four next week, and I am beginning to plan accordingly. Mommy is arranging for our birthday party to be at a teahouse called Tempest in a Teacup. A tea party! With strawberries and sandwiches with the crusts cut off, which is the only way Sara and I will eat them.

I also happen to know that there is a rat in the basement of our house, and where there's a rat in a nice suburban house, there's bound to be rat poison. I am dreaming of a felicitous conjunction between these two occurrences.

I want you to know that I don't plan to do in these little girls. That would be beyond the scope of my job description. I'm envisioning just a pinch of poison, enough to send everyone home with a tummy ache, have them puking up their birthday treats in their parents' cars.

I hope that my superiors notice my efforts here. I'll tell you the truth: I might have been getting a little complacent lately. Beelzebub actually sent me a reprimand last month because I hadn't been productive enough. I guess I've gotten into a rhythm, since I've been here so long. Kind of a mid-career plateau. I'm not as hungry, as ambitious, as I was as a young demon just starting out.

I believe the rat poison will please them. Meantime, Sara and I attend story hour at the public library. We dress our stuffed Pegasuses in doll clothes. We recite the list of little girls who have been invited to the party. That's a fun thing. Our favourite friends are all invited, and we like to say the guest list out loud to anyone who will listen. Libby, Bella, Emily, Alice. Suzie, Trixie, Eleanor, Rose.

One night we have a babysitter who lets us paint our fingernails and toenails pink and purple. Admiring my toenails, wiggling them while they dry, I can't remember the last time I was so delighted by something. Sara's pretty happy with hers, too. She lays her curly head on my shoulder and sighs, "You are my best friend."

The morning of the birthday party, Mommy lays our outfits on the beds. We are to wear velvet dresses with lace collars and pinafores. The pinafores each have a pocket, and that gives me an idea.

While we're supposed to be lying down for a nap, I whisper to Sara, "Let's go to the basement. I want to show you something. Bring your pinafore."

Up high on a shelf above the washing machine, beside the laundry soap, is a box of rat poison. Mommy thinks we can't get clear up here, but we can. Sara knows how to step in my hands for a boost up. She clambers onto the washer and pulls the box down for me. I pull off the lid and scoop a handful of poison out. "Here," I tell her, and I empty my hand into her little pinafore pocket. "Don't tell anybody."

"Okay," she says, always agreeable.

Off we go in the minivan to Tempest in a Teacup, gaily kicking our feet in our respective booster seats, singing "The Wheels on the Bus Go 'Round and 'Round" with Mommy.

Everyone is there, a cluster of little fairy princesses in pastel colours. Emily has insisted on wearing a tiara. I plan to burst into tears right before they bring out the cake and not stop sobbing until she lets me put it on. That's only a warm-up, though. After the cake, in the chaos of opening presents, I'll get Sara to go around and drop a little rat poison into each of the teacups. I'll tell her it's magic birthday sugar.

A funny thing happens during the party, though. First, the cake. It is frosted pink with a white frosting horse on top. It's made of angel food and layers of strawberries, and I've never tasted anything so marvelous. It occurs to me that this part of my job, this business of just being four, is better even than the opportunity for professional development. Then Sara and I open our first present. It's an eight-colour set of Play-Doh, and I just can't wait to get my pudgy little fingers into it. Sara cries, "Can we play with it right now?" and I see that she feels just the same way I do. We understand each other. Sara is my best friend. I realize I've blown my opportunity to spoil the cake with a fuss about the tiara, but I don't care, because the Play-Doh is from Emily and I love her for it. Suddenly I don't feel like poisoning her, or these other pretty creatures who are going to give me presents and play with me.

"Trade pinafores with me," I tell Sara.

"Why?" Sara is usually compliant, but it's her birthday, she's the star, and she's feeling a little uppity.

I have to think fast. "Mine is prettier," I tell her. "Look, you got strawberry on yours."

"Okay," she says, and we trade. I run off to the bathroom, empty the rat poison into the toilet, and flush it all away. When I return to the tearoom, I just watch. Nine four-year-old princesses are giggling and playing, their lips smeared with frosting, in the pastel paper kingdom of wrappers, paper and bows they've made. I don't go back. I turn and retreat to the bathroom and from there send myself straight to my higher-up's office.

"Mr. Beelzebub," I tell him, "I want a reassignment."

You couldn't ask for a gnarlier supervisor than Beelzebub. He thinks the sun shines out of his behind. Well, technically, it does. He's responsible for these heat waves we've been having lately. But anyway, he's there in his office, polishing his horns before the mirror, and he doesn't even look my way.

"Oh, you do, do you?" he says. "What's in it for me?"

"Name your price."

He sighs, runs a comb through his duckbill. "I have two hundred engine malfunctions to conjure by Thursday. Take them off my hands."

"Consider it done."

"All right then." Beelzebub pulls a file drawer open lazily and tosses an Excel printout on his desk. It's a list of all the posts for demons with my title, and the data associated with each. "Not much here," he says with indifference. "You could be a Young Republican."

"I'll take it," I say.

"Get the details from John," he says. "Bye-bye now."

John is the office manager; I pick up my new job description from him and in a matter of minutes am on my way to earth to swarm into the body of a twenty-three-year-old political activist. It pays the same as evil twinning. Perks include wealth and, if I stick with this guy long enough, potential for power. My first day on the job, I'm to attend a convention.

I can see right away there's not going to be much in the way of wonder and magic, though. The titles of the seminars I'm to attend are enough to make me nod off where I stand. I feel a pang, thinking of Sara—I miss her already—and at the same time a stab of confused guilt for having abandoned my post. Is this the right thing to do? Leaving the work I used to think was such a contribution, the work that kept me so fulfilled? Leaving Sara alone, without her best friend? No, this must be the right thing. Now Sara can have a normal childhood, undisturbed by voices in her head.

So here goes. This how I spend my day, trying to force my eyes to stay open. Surrounded by grey suits. The seminars are on development, on recent court rulings regarding "just compensation" for homeowners affected by eminent domain, on how individual property rights and market institutions provide the most effective realization of environmental protections…these guys don't need help from demons. I am going to be a fifth wheel in this job. I feel a little nauseous. And bored, bored, bored. At the end of the day, I've just about had it. My only consolation will be a trip to the sauna.

"That didn't last long," Beelzebub says dryly when I return.

"It wasn't my fault," I say. "He was murdered."

"So, shall I pass you on to the next Young Republican?"

"I've been thinking," I tell him. "I want to go back to being a doppelganger."

My supervisor looks me over. He starts to open his mouth, then apparently changes his mind. He gives a single nod. "Go," he says. "But I don't want to see you in here again for a good long time."

"I can promise it," I tell him.

On my way out the door, I pull off my demon badge and drop it on John's desk. "Don't say anything to anyone until I'm gone," I tell him, "but I'm resigning. I'm going to earth and not coming back."

John lifts and drops his eyebrows. "Whatever," he replies.

Sara drops the stuffed horse in her hands and runs to hug me when I come in. "Where did you go?" she says.

"Nowhere. It doesn't matter. I'm not going away again," I tell her. "And I'm going to be a good girl from now on, too."

Sara kisses me on the cheek. "Come on," she says. "Pegasus and I were just having tea."

Part 4

I can't believe how rude Americans are.

I had known in a general way that there were some problems of courtesy here. But until I arrived, I had no idea of the extent of it. The way people stared at me in the airport. The way they looked me over and whispered to their friends. The things they said right to my face! Not twenty-four hours in your country and I've been called shorty, pipsqueak, runt and shrimp; also, even less to my liking, elf, gremlin(!), and dwarf. A customs official asked me to remove my hat, which I found unspeakably offensive, and at the bar a woman actually ran her fingers through my beard. I suppose she was flirting with me. She said, "You're so cute! And I love your accent!" Your American courtship rituals leave a great deal to be desired.

They gave me a whole lot of trouble at customs. I couldn't have been more clear and straightforward about my intentions.

"Do you have a visa?" the officer asked me.

"I'm defecting," I announced. "I'm not going back. I am going to become an American citizen."

The customs officer gave me a long look of doubt. Then he called someone to come take me away to a little room, where I had to wait so long that I read both my mountaineering magazines cover to cover.

Then when he came back he made me explain myself all over again.

He sighed. "Sir?" he said. "You can't defect from Norway. If you want to immigrate, you can put in the paperwork like anyone else. You'll have to follow the proper channels."

I drew myself up to my full height, sixty-six centimetres. That's two feet, two inches to you Americans. I drew myself up, and I looked that customs officer in his indifferent eye, and I said, "You are obviously uninformed about the persecution of Norwegian Gnomes. My culture is under siege. I am not going back, and wild rabbits can't drag me."

The customs officer went to consult with someone else. The two of them stood outside the door talking in low voices, but not so low that the sharp ears of a Norwegian Forest Gnome couldn't make it out. I heard "mentally ill." I heard "harmless" and "unthreatening." I heard "quirky."

And then they came back in and said, "Sir? Your passport allows you to travel in America for a period of two weeks. That should give you enough time to begin the application process for immigration, should you choose to. However, be advised that if you overstay your time here, you will be in violation of the law."

And they sent me packing.

I had thought they would welcome me as a hero. I had thought there would be press conferences, interviews, photojournalists. Offers of hospitality. Offers of sponsorship.

What is America, if not the land that embraces and lifts up refugees? "Give me your tired, your poor, your huddled masses yearning to breathe free..." This is a bitter arrival indeed.

The insults had only begun. Faced with the prospect of Americanizing myself without a friend to guide me, I exited the airport and tried to hail a cab. I quickly discovered that Manhattan is just as bad as Oslo. Everything is geared to the tall. The cabbies couldn't—or wouldn't—even see me. In the end I had to clamber up onto a luggage cart to get attention.

Then the cab driver said to me, "Where you coming from? Santa's workshop?"

Maybe it's the way I'm dressed. I had put on my finest, of course, for the journey. My curly-toed shoes. My longest wool hat—it reaches past my knees. My embroidered jacket. I notice most everyone here is terribly underdressed. It's a rude, rude culture.

Or it could be all the things I'm carrying on my back that elicited the cabby's nasty taunt. I've come prepared for the great American wilderness. My backpack weighs as much as I do, and very proud I am to have the strength to hoist twenty-three kilos on my back. That's fifty-one pounds to you Americans.

I can rise above the insults. Soon Manhattan will be as far behind me as my native country. I am, after all, one of the Norwegian Forest Gnomes, known above all else as a people of dignity.

The train trip out west isn't especially comfortable. Your American train food is terrible. Crossing Tennessee, a conductor mistakes me for a child and picks me up. I have a little snit over it. He is very apologetic; I'll give him that. Crossing Kansas, a little girl spies me and wants me for a pet. I don't necessarily mind children, but this is too much. She cries and cries and her mother has to take her away to a different car.

I'll be glad to leave civilization behind.

My dream, you see, is to embrace the wilderness of the mighty American West. In Norway, the beloved forests of old are no more. It's all second growth, and the logging has had a devastating effect on Gnome culture. Most of us have lost our splendid heritage and become tame. Many have assimilated into Garden Gnome society. I watched it all happening before my eyes, and I decided to take a stand. If the habitat of the Forest Gnome is destroyed, why then, the Forest Gnome must take his culture elsewhere. Gnome culture must be preserved. I am the beginning of the Gnome Diaspora. We Forest Gnomes may have to wander the earth in search of the last wild places. But we Forest Gnomes will survive. We will survive.

My determination swells when the Rocky Mountains come into view. Such grandeur! Such unrivalled natural beauty! Such opportunity to reclaim and redignify my heritage! I open a window and fling my passport out.

The next day, I disembark in a Pacific Northwest town called Stevens' Ferry. Nestled in woods, it lies in the wilds of the Cascade Mountain range, the promised land. Gnome pride wells up in me. I will backpack from the trailhead just outside of town, deep into the forest.

I don't feel ready to begin just yet, though. Standing at the gateway to the National Forest, sizing up the road ahead and with the pretty little town behind me, I feel I should refuel. It's a short trek into town to a corner grocery. I buy a loaf of homemade artisan bread there and some other supplies. The grocer doesn't say a word about my size or my attire. Maybe folks are more polite out here in the west, or maybe it's the small-town ethos.

Across the street a child is playing in the grass of her front yard. She looks to be about four, my girth but about twice my height.

"Hi," she says. "Wanna play?"

I consider. She's having tea in the garden. I don't mind telling you, I like a cup of tea, and I like gardens.

"Very well," I tell her. "Some ground rules. No picking me up."

"Okay," she says.

"And hands off the beard."

"Okay. What's your name?"

"Edvard."

"That's a funny name."

Do you see what I mean? Rude, rude, rude.

"My name is Sara. My sister is Sally. She went away."

"That's a pity. Do you have any milk?" I ask.

Sara, an obliging hostess, pours imaginary milk into my teacup. Very dear, really.

We nibble in silence for a bit.

"What are you afraid of?" Sara asks me suddenly.

This is not a question I have often pondered. "Big animals," I tell her after a time. I was mauled by a rabbit before. It ate up my hat and part of my beard, and I tell you, I hardly lived through the fright. "What are you afraid of?"

"Being alone," she says.

After tea I shake Sara's hand. "It was a pleasure to make your acquaintance," I tell her. "We must have tea again, should I ever pass this way in future."

It's not a bad place, this town. A good place to set out from. I doubt, of course, that I will pass this way again, because I am a Norwegian Forest Gnome, on my way to becoming a Wild American Mountain Gnome. I shoulder my pack with a sense of great beginnings, spit-polish the hand-carved marmot head atop my walking stick, and set out.

I'm not twenty steps away when Sara runs up behind me. "Edvard!"she cries. "Don't go." Her blue eyes are very big and are beginning to puddle up with tears.

"Oh, my dear," I tell her, strangely sad to be leaving behind my only American friend. "I must go. It's my destiny."

"What's destiny?"

"What is meant to happen," I tell her. "I am meant to go live in the mountains."

She studies me a long time, as though she doubts me. It crosses my mind that such boldness is another example of how improperly children are brought up this side of the Atlantic.

"If you get lonely, you can come back and live with me," Sara says. "You can pretend to be my sister."

"That's very kind of you," I tell her, wanting to wriggle away from this conversation. "Good day."

It's a lot of work, backpacking. Quickly I'm sweaty under my wool. I remove my good hat and tuck it away. Then my good jacket. A few miles in and my feet are really beginning to hurt me. Also, I'm not very happy about the effect the trail is having on my curly-toed shoes. It's possible I should have invested in a pair of hiking boots. It hurts my pride, though, that my feet are not naturally adept at this endeavour. I assumed they would be.

Time for a little snack. Some bread and cheese are in order. I'd really like a tomato to go with this, too, but they don't pack very well, so I didn't bring any. A painful thought crosses my mind, which is that out here in the mighty wilderness, I will have to forage for my own food. My ancestors lived on a diet of berries and nuts, quail's eggs and wild mushrooms. I know I can do it. I might even shed a few of these extra pounds I've been lugging around. Still, I realize I'm going to miss my Camembert.

A snack restores my vigour, and the sight and smell of the great Douglas fir trees swaying above me reminds me of the nobility of my mission. Onward and upward.

Evening brings with it a new set of problems. I've managed to pitch my tent and have unrolled my sleeping bag inside. But for the life of me I am unable to get a fire started. My feet are cold, my hands are stiff. I eat an unsatisfying cold meal of day-old artisan bread—leaving only the heel for breakfast—and the last of my Camembert, and I curl up in a ball in my sleeping bag, feeling rather miserable.

I did not realize living in the woods would be so unpleasant. I thought only of how rugged I would become, how ennobled in the presence of Nature.

All right, I will make a confession to you.

I have never lived in the Norwegian forests.

I am a Garden Gnome. I am one of the assimilated. Born and raised in a cottage garden in an Oslo suburb. Raised, mind you, on tales of the forest life we Gnomes used to lead. Raised on bitterness over the felling of the once magnificent Norwegian wilds. But never so much as sent away to summer camp. Never taken on a day hike. Suckled on the sour milk of nostalgia and imagination.

How piteous am I! Oh, and how far from home! I am sniffling now in my tent, and shivering with cold. I curl up, fetal and pathetic, until I am deeply disgusted with myself.

In the wee hours of the morning I sit up in my tent and give myself a stern talking-to. Edvard, I say. You are by ancestry a Norwegian Forest Gnome. Your whole self-worth is on the line here. And not only yours. The dignity of your whole people is at stake. Find your inner strength. Face your fears! Rise to the occasion! Grow!

I go like this until I have regained my composure and my determination. Tomorrow I will set out to find berries and wild mushrooms. Tomorrow I will teach myself to build a fire. Tomorrow I will climb, growing ever stronger and more resilient. Climb high! Climb to the summit! Soar!

Peaceful at last, I am just about to lie back down when I hear thumping in the woods. It must be wild beasts. Huge ones, from the sound of it. A whole tromping herd. I unzip the tent flap just a bit and peek out. Through the trees and brush beyond my campsite I see movement. Figures, tall as humans, but stiff and ponderous in their gait. There must be a dozen or more, and they're headed this way. As they draw nearer I see them in the moonlight. They're pale white, almost green, ghastly of complexion and glassy-eyed, arms outstretched and moving with dreadful certainty over the forest floor. They're making an unholy ruckus, too; birds and small mammals are skittering away in their path. From time to time they moan at one another. Yet they don't seem to notice me, and they shuffle by, a strange herd. I watch them until they're out of sight, then continue to squat here, tense, ready to flee, until they're out of hearing.

The forests of America are filled with strangenesses with which I never imagined I would contend. I badly want to get off this mountain now, but where would I go? I should try to sleep, or at least to rest, and gather my courage once again.

I'm just about to drift off in the early hours of the morning when I hear another scuffling outside my tent. Without cover of darkness, I feel horribly exposed. Quiet as I can, I wriggle out of my sleeping bag and pull my curly-toed shoes on, so I can make a break for it, if need be. Just then a snout appears in the unzipped flap of my tent, a great, terrible black snout, which pushes into my space; a furry white face appears, half as big as myself, and a pair of leering eyes, and then a pair of horns. A high, involuntary squeal issues from my mouth, and before I am aware of taking action, I have seized the stale heel of my loaf of artisan bread and chucked it dead ahead. The mountain goat backs out of my tent. I jump up and scramble out. The goat is there, monstrous, terrible. Do mountain goats eat Gnomes? Is this beast my natural predator? I am not about to find out. I take the only sensible option, and I turn and run, run, pattering across the campsite and back to the trail as fast as my curly-toed shoes will carry me, down the trail, down, down, over tree roots, over creeks, leaving my tent and my pack behind me, leaving my walking stick with the hand-carved marmot head, leaving my visions of grandeur, my dreams, leaving the promised land. I don't stop running until I've retraced every step of yesterday, until I've come to the trailhead and the familiar town of Stevens' Ferry.

This is for the best, really. I've settled into my new home now. Sara and her family have allowed me to live on their property. Evidently Sara's sister has come back, but they let me stay anyway—and it's a relief to me that I don't have to pretend to be little Sally. I've kept the best of my heritage: my good hat, my embroidered jacket. I can still enjoy the fruits of nature, here in the garden, under the beefsteak tomatoes. I've combed the thistles out of my beard and reclaimed my dignity. Sara comes outside for a tea party now and again. I am an American Garden Gnome now, proud to inhabit a garden in sight of the mountains of the great American West. And my journey here was an achievement. For the rest of my days, I can look back on my moment of heroism: the day I hiked up into the mighty Cascades, was nearly trampled by a herd of monsters, and faced down a Gnome-eating mountain goat. For the rest of my days, I will have that tale to tell.

you find out who your true friends are when you have seventeen cats.

Once, my house was the place to be. I had friends, friends of friends, acquaintances, cousins, visitors coming and going all the time. We had an open door, always. Hospitality. Generosity. These were values that I thought were universally held as dear. But you open your doors to the wrong kind, and you find out differently. These days, my friends, my relatives, even my own coven members seem to find excuses not to drop by. They claim my house smells. They complain about cats landing with a thud, as though from the sky, in the middle of the dining table while we're eating. As though cats don't get hungry, too. As though cats were second-class citizens. The last time Hecate was here, I asked her what she was planning to wear to the Solstice party, and she held up her sleeves and said, "Well, it looks like I'm wearing your cats." Yes, orange hair does show on a black dress. I'm not ashamed. I'm a witch. I wear cat hair with pride.

I saw Hecate tonight at the City Commission meeting. We were there to speak in favour of a proposal to bury the power lines in Stevens' Ferry. It's a good idea, from our point of view, because power lines pose a threat to low-flying broomstick riders. But of course we can't say that in a City Commission meeting, so we slipped in among the environmentalists and neighbourhood association members who were there to lobby for the proposal on health and aesthetic grounds. The mayor and the other commissioners were clucking about the cost, and I left the meeting discouraged, certain it wouldn't be approved. I caught Hecate at the door and asked her if she'd like to come over for tea, but she looked sideways and said, "No, I've got to be running along. Power Night coming up," and she threw me a certain look of warning.

Oh, yeah, that. I'd forgotten about the full moon. The cats have been taking so much of my energy lately that I haven't been doing a lot of witchcraft.

Two of my familiars are waiting where my broomstick is parked, behind the public library where City Commission meetings take place. They jump onto my shoulders, and I straddle my broom and murmur the usual incantation for take-off: "Fair is foul and foul is fair; hover through fog and filthy air." It's a little outdated, since state emissions-reduction legislation means our air is relatively clean.

Anyway, flying home, I pass over a trio of hairy men with their arms around each other, singing, obviously in their cups. Nights with bright moons aren't my favourite nights to be out. I haven't heard about any witches in town getting eaten, but I can imagine a desperate werewolf wouldn't say no to cat flesh.

The drunken men must notice me veering away from them on my broom, because one of them calls after me, "Don't worry, sister! There's enough moon to go around!"

Well, I'm not taking advantage of the moon tonight, nearly full or not. I need to keep Mack out of trouble, and besides, the cats needs their claws trimmed.

When I get home, Mack is sitting on the living room floor, his back up against the bookcase, picking lint out of his belly button with a pair of tweezers. "Look what I found," he says when he sees me, holding up an unsavoury tidbit.

"Mack, that's disgusting."

My brother cackles and goes back to his hunt.

"Did you go to the unemployment office today?"

"I missed the bus," Mack says without looking away from his navel. "I'll go tomorrow."

Many of our conversations include this particular exchange. "There's a bus every ten minutes," I say. "You could get to the unemployment office if you wanted to."

"My left elbow was bothering me," says Mack. "I'll go tomorrow."

Mack came to stay "just for a few days" nine months ago, saying he needed a place to crash until he found a job. I can't blame employers for not wanting

44

him, but he hasn't tried very hard. He'd been driving a beer delivery truck over in Pleasant Grove until he got fired for helping himself to the cargo. And do you suppose he makes any kind of contribution around here? Has he ever once brewed a potion or cleaned out a litter box?

The kitchen resembles a federally declared disaster site from what looks to have been an afternoon pizza spree. "Aw, hell," I mutter, and push my sleeves up. Looks like I'll be spending the evening casting cleaning spells.

I'm combing Mr. Cutepaws a few nights later when I get the unpleasant phone call. "Margot," says the deep voice I know so well. "Hecate here."

"Hey there!" I say, all sunny, but as my voice trails away I realize it's not a social call.

"Where were you last night?"

I clap my hand to my forehead. "Oh, my Goddess," I say. "Power Night. I completely forgot."

"It's not the first time, Margot. And there are people depending on you."

"I know. I'm so sorry. I had to give the cats their hairball treatments and I just completely lost track of the days. It won't happen again."

"It can't happen again. I have to tell you, there are going to be serious consequences for you if you don't straighten yourself out. I'm not just speaking for myself here."

Hecate lets the implication hang heavy in the air.

"Okay," I whisper. "I understand."

I'm getting to be as bad as Mack. I could never look at myself in the mirror again if I thought I was becoming such an unreliable sack of toad pus.

At the same time, I feel misunderstood. My coven sisters have no idea how much work it takes to care for this many cats, and they don't seem to appreciate what a service to society it is. Can't they cut me some slack?

As I mull this over, I'm certain I hear an owl screech outside. That could definitely be a sign. Of what, though? Sometimes it's tricky to divine. It could be a bad omen: I've blown it with my coven. On the other hand, it could simply be a warning, reinforcing Hecate's message: I should watch my step. Or, it could just be an owl screeching.

I'm extra careful to do my share for the next few weeks. It's my job to take care of inventory, and during this time I'm mindful to keep amulets and love potions, incantation songsheets, and spell kits in stock. I spend an afternoon picking mugwort for our herbarium. I even get some paint and touch up the faded pentagram on the wall behind the ping-pong table in the community centre. And here's the thanks I get: one night at a coven meeting—and I haven't missed a single meeting in a month—the whole group pretty much snubs me.

Things start out well enough. Hecate calls the meeting to order as always: "How now, thou secret, black and midnight hags. What is it you do?"

And we all answer in unison, "A deed that has no name," and then Hecate passes out the agenda. Old business: the City Commission voted down the power lines proposal because of unexpected demands on the city's budget. New business: we're hosting a visiting Druid; is anyone willing to put her up for a couple nights?

"I will," I say. "I'd be happy to." I have a big house, and everyone knows how I love to extend my hospitality.

All my coven sisters look at each other.

"I don't think that's such a good idea," says Morgan.

"It's my understanding that Druids don't really care for cats," pipes Guinevere.

"And then there's your brother," adds Hecate.

Diana says, "It's not really the welcome we want to extend to an honoured guest."

I am crushed. "Well, I'll have the place clean, obviously," I tell them.

They look dubious and uncomfortable. "Your cats are kind of...ubiquitous," Morgan says.

I can't believe my ears. "What kind of self-respecting witches have a problem with a few cats?"

They look at each other. "A dozen is more than a few," Hecate points out.

"Seventeen, actually," I snap. They all give each other a knowing look. "Whatever," I tell them. Druids make really boring houseguests anyway.

"So, Mack?"

Mack is lying on his stomach in the kitchen, tracing the patterns in the linoleum with one finger. "Unh," he says.

"Did you go to the unemployment office today?"

"It's not open on Saturdays."

"Today is Tuesday."

"Oh. Today is Tuesday? I thought it was Saturday."

"No." I open my mouth to tell him what else I'm thinking about him, but the cats have noticed I'm home and they fairly ambush me. We go around the kitchen counter to their food dishes, the seventeen cats and I. "Did you not even notice that their bowls were empty?" I ask Mack, disgusted.

Not taking his eyes off the linoleum, Mack says, "Whose bowls?"

I'm supposed to attend another City Commission meeting, but I don't have the heart for it. Modern witchcraft requires far too many committee meetings. Instead I stay home, rubbing Mumblypeg's tummy, scratching Greymalkin around the ears, and trying to figure out a way to get my brother to get a job and start paying rent. I can't just kick him out, now, can I? What would he do with himself?

Next day in the paper I read that Stevens' Ferry is experiencing a terrible rat infestation. It's driving tourists away and creating a health hazard, and is going to be expensive to confront. Mayor Bajolaluna attributes it, perhaps euphemistically, to inadequate garbage collection; the word on the street is that the real problem is the improper disposal of human remains. Body parts keep turning up in ordinary household trashcans and dumpsters behind commercial sites.

Some of my cats have ear mites, and I spend the day performing auricular lavage on them with a plastic bulb, a towel and a vast number of cotton swabs. Mack lies on the floor and watches. "I wish we had furniture," he says. I've gotten rid of my sofa and most of my chairs in the last year or two to make space for cat-climbing structures, carpeted windowsill shelves, and cat beds.

"You could get a job and buy yourself some," I growl.

"Is there anything to eat?" he asks as though I haven't said anything.

"You could get up and go look in the cupboards for yourself."

"Oh." Mack doesn't move.

So apparently, one of my neighbours has filed a complaint about the cats. She doesn't care for their singing, evidently. I receive a notice to this effect from the city. That night when they strike up their nightly moon-howls, I stand out by the back fence and sing with them.

Next night I'm out on my broomstick, cruising over fields of pumpkins and half-heartedly chanting an incantation for a favourable autumn harvest, when I'm certain I hear the whine of a hedge-pig. It must be significant, but in what way? I hear the whine repeated one, two, three, four times. "Thrice and once the hedge-pig whin'd!" It's a sign, but what can it mean? What can it mean?

Uneasy, I tilt homeward, leaving the harvest chants incomplete. When I reach my house I find eleven broomsticks leaning against the railing of my front porch. I have company.

All my coven members are in my living room, sitting on the floor among the climbing structures, waiting for me.

"What a surprise!" I cry with forced cheer. "My birthday's not until November!"

They look awfully grim, these women in black.

"Have a seat," says Diana. "We need to talk."

"What's on your mind?" I scoop the brinded cat Aloysius (named for our city's founding father) into my arms.

"We're here to do an intervention," says Hecate.

I'm stunned into silence. There is no sound but that of Aloysius purring.

"It's your cats," Hecate continues. "You have too many. Things can't go on this way."

"Says who?"

"They're interfering with your work," Diana says. "They're distracting you, keeping you from pulling your weight."

"We considered asking you to leave the coven," Guinevere puts in, "but then we realized that you have a problem. You need help, Margot."

Hecate goes on, "Cat collecting is a form of obsessive-compulsive disorder."

"My cats are my family! I would think you, of all people, would understand that!"

"You can't take care of a family this big. If you love them, you'll consider letting some of them go to other homes where they can get everything they need."

"Nonsense! They're my familiars!"

"No one has seventeen familiars, Margot. That's completely unorthodox. It's an abuse of the system."

This outrageous poppycock goes on for some time until I am practically hissing and spitting. For the first time in my life, I feel inhospitable. I have never turned anyone away from my door before, much less asked anyone to leave my home. Yet I am offended to the marrow by this betrayal. I turn these events over and over in my mind, while the members of my coven are going on about

49

my falling behind in cataloguing wool of bat, about the cost of cat food these days, about how people sometimes behave irrationally under stress. Then suddenly Aloysius mews, three times. "Thrice the brinded cat hath mew'd!" This is always a meaningful sign. I gaze into Aloysius's yellow eyes. I know what I must do: act in his best interest, and that of his siblings.

"I need all of you to go away right now," I tell my coven sisters in what I hope is a quiet but terrible voice. In short order they gather up their cloaks and move to the door. They tell me I can't come back to the coven until I've given up all but two cats (neutered!) and am in therapy.

Well, I wouldn't go back if they begged me.

A few minutes after they're gone, the doorbell rings. It's a pizza delivery service. Mack answers, and, while the delivery boy is still standing there holding the pizza, Mack opens the box and helps himself to a slice.

"That'll be sixteen-fifty, sir," says the delivery boy.

Mack, his mouth full of pizza and mozzarella hanging down to his chin, simply points at me.

The triple mew of Aloysius is still echoing in my mind. After the pizza delivery kid is gone, I tell Mack, "This is it. I can't afford to support you any more. I'm giving you two weeks to find someplace to live and something to live on."

Mack sucks the dangling string of mozzarella up into his mouth with an ugly sound. "You're just mad because your girlfriends are bitches," he says. "Don't take it out on me."

"I mean it, Mack."

But he's already turned his back on me, trudging off to his room, pizza box under his arm.

The next day I rise before dawn and drive my pickup truck way out to the bog to catch newts. Eye of newt is hard to come by, because it's so labour-intensive to harvest. I figure I can market it to the other covens in town. Plus, I hear another new coven is being formed because of recent population growth in

Stevens' Ferry, and they'll need start-up supplies. They might even let me join them, although right now I'm considering self-employment; I don't want to get burned again. So to speak.

When I get home—cold, wet, tired, and having worked a sixteen-hour day in the bog—there's a notice in my mailbox from Animal Control. It has come to the city's attention that I have more domestic pets than is permitted by city ordinance. I have two weeks to reduce the number of my cats to five (the city of Stevens' Ferry is more reasonable, I guess, than my coven members). If I am noncompliant, I am subject to a fine and/or seizure of my property, i.e., said cats.

The City of Stevens' Ferry does not know from noncompliant. The City of Stevens' Ferry has never messed with Margot Gatto.

Two weeks pass. I change all the locks on my house. I'm inside baking catnip turnovers when I hear Mack rattling the doorknob. Then he starts to bang and shout my name. I have never in my life not answered my door before.

I ignore him.

Later, an Animal Control jeep pulls up to the house. An officer in uniform knocks on the door, waits, knocks, waits. The cats and I enjoy our snack. The officer goes away.

The new coven pays cash for a truckload of newt eyes, netting me enough to get through to Halloween, if I'm frugal. They seem nice, too: Blackberry Coven, they call themselves.

Downtown one afternoon, I stumble on some kind of demonstration taking place in the plaza. I'm standing on tiptoes to try and see what it's all about when I spot my brother in the crowd.

"Mack," I say, approaching him. "What's going on?"

"The Shitty Commission is slashing our arts budget," Mack tells me. "They say they have to use the money to clean up the rat problem. We say Bajolaluna's the real rat."

"Who's 'we'?"

Mack gestures at a sizable group of protestors, chanting and carrying signs. His own sign reads, Poetry, not poison.

This sudden fit of social consciousness on Mack's part is highly suspicious. "You don't give a rip about the arts," I say.

"I am a great aficionado of the arts," says Mack, striking what I guess is meant to be a dignified pose, lifting his pug nose into the air.

"Name one art of which you are an aficionado. Name one art, period."

I notice that the protestors have set up a tent city in the plaza. My guess is that they're planning to camp out here until the city restores its arts funds. And Mack is tagging along because, by pretending to be an activist, he gets a tent, a sleeping bag and supporter-provided food for the duration of the protest.

"I won't play your games, Margot," he tells me. "You kicked me out of your life, remember? I don't have to answer to you any more."

Like he ever did. "You're a pathetic fraud and a mooch," I tell him. "You're taking advantage of these people's sincerity. Did you get them to give you a tent and sleeping bag?"

"No," he tells me in an affronted tone. "I provided my own."

"Since when have you owned camping gear?"

Mack simply turns away from me. I walk off, disgusted. Just before I leave the plaza, I turn and see my brother crawling into his tent. It's tiny, like a tent for a child or a doll, and it has a Norwegian flag on one side. Goddess only knows where he got it.

According to the newspaper, the rat problem has become so severe that the City Commission has cancelled Stevens' Ferry's annual Poetry Slam, a season of city-sponsored theatre, and numerous dance scholarships for young people, in order to pay for exterminators. A lot of citizens are upset.

But I have problems of my own. When I get home, a uniformed officer is waiting for me on my porch. She says she is authorized to search my home and impound my cats. "I'll burn at the stake first!" I scream, and I daze her momentarily with a dazing spell, giving me enough time to get inside and barricade the door with a cat-climbing structure. It's a standoff. Police come. They talk to me with a megaphone. They try to coax me out. They say they won't harm the cats. They say it's for the best.

It occurs to me that in the past, blinded by my own attachment to the value of hospitality, I allowed myself to be bullied and taken advantage of. But no longer. The triple mew of Aloysius was a triple call to action. I will overcome my attachment in three ways: by denying my home to my coven, to my brother, and to the law.

Night falls. I crawl into the kitchen—I don't want them to see my silhouette— but I can't find anything to eat but catnip and stale pizza crusts. It's okay. I can hold out.

Aloysius joins me on the linoleum. He cleans his stripey yellow fur, then leaps onto the kitchen counter and sits there like a sphinx.

I begin to reflect. Me, I can hold out for a week, ten days—but how long can the cats hold out? They've got a few days' worth of food here at best. And what about their litter boxes? My heart sinks.

It's late. I peer out the window and see police officers leaning against their patrol cars, looking weary. Aloysius jumps down from the kitchen counter and onto my lap. I pet him for a while, and then ask him what I should do, and he mews three times.

It's a clear sign.

I go around and pet and praise each of the seventeen cats. Then I open the door and go out with my hands up.

The darkest hour of my life to date is spent handcuffed in the back seat of a patrol car, watching that Animal Control officer cart away my family members in twos and threes.

I spend the night in jail, wide awake, thinking. They let me go in the morning, but not before they fine me seventy-five dollars for the trouble I caused.

I don't go home; I go straight to City Hall, to the office of Mayor Esperanza Bajolaluna. She receives me and listens respectfully to what I have to say. In the end, we strike a deal.

And that is how Stevens' Ferry gets rid of its rat problem, through the services of seventeen cats formerly under the guardianship of Margot Gatto. And how the city of Stevens' Ferry restores its entire arts budget and saves the beloved annual Poetry Slam, an entire season of theatre including a fall production of Guys and Dolls, and the careers of several budding dancers. It is also how sixteen members of the newly formed Blackberry Coven come to have cats, of which they were sorely in need. (Aloysius stays on with me as my familiar, and we visit the others frequently.) It is how Mack gets enrolled in a course on self-reliance and acquires his own basement apartment. And how I save myself seventy-five dollars, which I put toward a new living-room sofa, and get my picture in the paper as a local hero of sorts. "What do you think of all that, buddy?" I ask Aloysius, who's sitting on my shoulder while we fly, and the yellow brinded cat begins to purr.

Samuel and I are really starting to worry about Isadora. She's always been a magnificent creature: tall, big-boned, her hair long and silken. But lately she's taken to weighing herself two or three times a day, skipping meals, and studying herself in the mirror for hours. She's endlessly trying on clothes. "Horizontal stripes will balance my width-height ratio," she tells me. "Pleated pants will give me a more defined waistline." And other nonsense of this kind. It's these teen magazines, they come to the house and Isadora treats them like manuals. If she devoted half the time studying for her SATs that she spends poring over these advice rags, she'd be headed for the Ivy League. The miserable fact is that she will never look a thing like these publications say she should. She doesn't have the genes for it. Obviously. It breaks my heart to see her longing for something she so clearly can never have. And shouldn't want. Why, she's a natural beauty. Any young Sasquatch man would be thrilled to have our daughter at his side.

I'm the brokenhearted mother, and Samuel just gets testy. "I'm going to tear down those posters," he says. Isadora's got posters on her wall of human fashion models, little bitty hairless things with bones like pretzel sticks. "I'm going to tear up those magazines."

"You'll just drive her away," I tell him. "What she needs is compassion."

"I'm going to break the bathroom scales," says Samuel.

It didn't used to be like this. Izzy was spunky as a grade-schooler. She ran and jumped, climbed trees and played dodgeball, just like all the other boys and girls. She didn't have any image problems. Around the time she started middle school, she got fussy about her hair, but even then, she seemed fine with her physique. It's only in the last few months that this obsession's grown—since we moved, I suppose, and she had to change schools.

I've noticed that she's started hunching her shoulders. I want to tell her that hunching doesn't make her any smaller; it just makes her look sloppy and like a person with low self-esteem. Of course, she has low self-esteem. Oh, my beautiful girl. How could she think herself so unlovely? "Honey, your posture," I can't keep from saying. She scowls at me. I can't help it; I'm worried. It can't be good for her back to go around slumping like that. And a Sasquatch woman should stand tall, stand proud! Classically hirsute and dark, Isadora has the magnificent broad shoulders, the fine large hands, and the strong thick neck of the most beautiful women of her generation. It's a terrible waste that she longs to be diminutive and pale.

"We should do something to instill Sasquatch pride in her," I tell Samuel. I start bringing home biographies of famous Bigfoot women and casually leave them lying around. Samuel buys us all tickets to the Bigfoot Women's Mudwrestling Competition at the Stevens' Ferry County Fair.

"I'm not going," Isadora says, crossing her arms. "You can't make me."

We go without her. Later I find out that this same night the Miss America pageant was on television. She must have wanted to stay home to watch it.

"I'm going to break the TV," Samuel says.

Samuel and I have had troubles of our own. We have this new house and we haven't sold our old one yet. That makes money tight, and we get into tangles about it. I just started a new job as the director of the Stevens' Ferry Museum, and I'm still learning the ropes. Then one of our new neighbours told us she had rats in her basement. If we get rats, I will die. Samuel said not to worry about it, that rats would probably be drawn to human houses because of the smell.

That's another thing that's stressful: we've moved into a mixed human-Sasquatch neighbourhood. Of course I think it's a good, progressive thing, and all our neighbours are perfectly nice people, but it's an adjustment. Some of Isadora's classmates this year are these little slips of people with no hair. I suppose it's natural that she's concerned about fitting in with her new crowd. "Just be yourself, honey," I advise her. She looks at me with such disdain that I hurry out of the room.

No Small Feet

And then there's Samuel's job. With the city's budget problems, he's been going to extra meetings and it seems we hardly see each other. One week we both work late every night. By Friday, I'm concerned. We've hardly spoken, except to compare work schedules, and we haven't been intimate in I don't know how long.

I try to approach it with humour. "Howdy, stranger," I tell him when he crawls under the covers. "Remind me what your name is?"

Samuel is in no mood to be jollied. "City Commissioners have big responsibilities," he tells me. "You knew it would be like this when you agreed to my running for office."

"Marriages can die of neglect, you know," I say. He just sighs and rolls away from me.

The next morning I walk in on Isadora in the bathroom, and she's spraying dreadful hair removal product on her legs. "What in heaven's name?" I say. Naturally she has long hair all over her legs, her arms, her chest, her lovely face. She is going to look utterly ridiculous if she takes it off.

"Honey, no," I tell her. "You're going to regret it. It won't look right."

"You don't know what you're talking about," she snaps. "It's not 1985 any more, Mother."

"But, sweetheart—"

"Get out of my life!" my daughter cries.

That night Samuel and have a big fight. "I think it's time we looked into therapy," I tell him. "Maybe a group for adolescent girls."

"I think it's time we looked into a good swift kick in the pants," Samuel says.

I'm appalled at his lack of understanding, and he acts disgusted with me. We do a thing we've never done in our marriage before: we go to bed mad.

It gets worse. A few days later, I come upon Isadora wrapping her feet in athletic tape. "Did you hurt yourself, honey?" I asked. But I know from the look on her face I am being naïve. She was binding her feet.

A Bigfoot's feet should be her pride and joy!

"This has got to stop," I tell her gently. I think she's going to spew more venom, but instead she bursts out crying.

"Mama," she cries. "Why can't I be petite?" She lays her silky head on my shoulder and sobs.

It is my most heartrending moment in sixteen years of mothering.

Samuel and I have had an offer on the old house, and we have to go see the real estate agent about it. We talk on the way over. "Look," he says to me. "Maybe we should just back off. We've been so worked up about this thing with Izzy—you're worried, and I'm pissed off. Maybe if we make less of a big deal of it, she won't feel she has to cling to it so hard."

He could be right. It's worth a try, anyway. So when we come home again—in pretty good spirits, since it looks like we're going to sell the house—and Isadora announces she wants to spend the summer at ballet camp, well, we let her.

I secretly think it's a terrible idea. She wants to develop gracefulness. But she's going to seem so very awkward dancing alongside a bunch of little willowy human ballerinas. Doesn't she see it? I want to protect her from the humiliation. But Isadora is nothing if not stubborn. She's determined to go. And I already agreed with Samuel that I would try to mellow out. So I bite my tongue, and let my six-foot-four, hundred-seventy-pound daughter pack her bags and go away to ballet camp.

The weeks go by. We get postcards, but no real sense of how she's doing. I'm worried about Isadora, but I keep quiet about it. I want to keep the peace with Samuel. Work helps to distract me: the security guard quit with no notice—claiming he'd seen a ghost, or a statue come to life, or some such nonsense—so I had to find a replacement for him right away. I also try to keep my mind off Izzy by making friends with the neighbours. I have to admit it—a new job, a new house, a new neighbourhood—it doesn't feel like home yet.

Remind me why we did this? I say to myself sometimes. I know, I know: the museum job is a good one, the neighbourhood has a great school, and the picture window in the living room frames a mountain view.

One evening, my husband comes home unexpectedly early. We sit at the dining table to have a talk. "Look," he says. "I know Izzy's absence has been hard on you. You've been great. I figured I could do more, too. So—I resigned from the budget committee, I resigned from the power line committee, and I told them I'm not being a judge in the tomato competition this year. We need our weeknights back, you and I."

"Samuel!"

"You know what else?" he tells me. "I've been kind of a jerk. I'll do better. I'll be nicer to you and Izzy. Okay?"

He's been playing footsie with me under the table as he talks. I think my mouth is hanging open, because he starts to chuckle at my expression. "And you know what else?" he says. Then he grabs my hand and we practically run upstairs, shedding clothes as we go. It's been a long time since we were this enthusiastic, and, thumping up the steps behind him, I realize I'd forgotten how much I appreciate those big noisy feet of his, and that muscled, furry little tush.

At the end of the summer, Isadora sends a letter.

"Dear Mama and Daddy," it reads. "I want to write and tell you about exciting developments at dance camp.

"Things didn't go so well in ballet. I was determined, and I worked hard. But my instructor said that in ballet, determination and hard work are ninety percent of what you need, but the other ten percent is the right body type and, well, I just don't have it. But she said I obviously have what it takes to be a dancer!—just not a ballet dancer. She recommended me to the modern dance instructor, and I moved over to modern dance. I love it! And Mama, Daddy, the city of Stevens' Ferry has offered me a scholarship to attend a professional dance academy in New York City!!!! They've told me that with my build, and especially with my feet, I could really make a name for myself in modern dance. If I work hard. Which I will, I promise!"

Samuel and I hardly know what to say to each other, we are so amazed. Amazed, and welling up with pride for our bigfooted daughter, who is being herself in a bigger way than we ever imagined she could. We read the letter over again, and then sit together in silence, gazing out the picture window of our home, and Samuel takes my hand.

It gets old, having to explain myself all the time.

I mean, you never hear in casual conversation, "A witch. Now, what is that again?" No one says to an acquaintance, "Vampiring—tell me how that works." Nobody, when the Abominable Snowman comes in on the arm of one of his innumerable girlfriends, asks the lucky woman, "And who do we have here?"

But when I go out in public, when I have to be introduced, there's always this confusion. First the furtive glances, the discomfort, the straining to overlook my texture. Then, when it all comes out, the disconcertedness. The way no one understands, even when I explain it politely. It's hard, being the only one of me.

Just this week, for instance, I'm at an office party, and they've just hired this woman in accounting. Owen, who works in my department, is making the rounds with her. He's either oblivious to all this awkwardness or is very good at hiding his feelings. "Barney," he says in his usual cheerful way, "I'd like to introduce you to our newest hire." I've watched the way humans take a new person around and touch the old person and new person on their shoulders as they say so-and-so, this is so-and-so. The way the so-and-so's shake hands and make small talk with big smiles and interested eyes. Nobody touches my shoulders, of course, and I don't mind at all; it's not that. I don't mind that the new accountant doesn't shake my hand. What bothers me is the moment of poorly disguised shock in her face. And the way she starts to extend her hand and then pulls it back, and then thinks she's being rude and extends it again, only to realize finally and with relief that I'm not offering mine. Then she stands with both hands behind her back just in case. In her face I can see a whole mini-drama of opposing forces, the fear behind the plasticity of her smile and politically correct attentiveness. She is mute, struggling within herself.

"What's your name?" I ask pleasantly. The new accountant has an abundance of curly black hair and a pointy, perceptive-looking face.

"Julia. And you're...Barney?"

Gerald is my given name, but most of my office mates call me Barney. It's an affectionate nickname, and I appreciate being included in their affection, I really do. But I would like to be more than Barnacle Man. I'm a whole person. I have skills. I have dreams. I am more than my barnacles.

"Barney's our head tech writer," says Owen. If I were human, Owen would be giving me a friendly slap on the back, but of course he doesn't want lacerations, so he lifts his plastic wineglass in the gesture of a toast instead. "One of the best."

Owen means well, but it's these sorts of interactions that make me feel I'm being worn as a badge of honour, so everyone can see how progressive the company is. They always act like they adore me. But it's always from a distance. They adore me, but they don't know me.

"Interesting," Julia says, looking more interested in making a dash for it than in discussing my career. "I'm sure our paths will cross again." She gives a wan little smile and slips away into the crowd.

I can't judge any of them. It's not their fault. I'm just tired, that's all. And lonely.

Next day in my office cubicle I find myself sighing and distracted. I wouldn't mind a more sociable job. Tech writing's okay, but it's solitary work, and then I go home to an empty apartment, to my Sudoku and my poetry. My therapist has been encouraging me to get out more, and I know he's right. He used to be more sympathetic, but lately he's been kind of pushy. I think he believes it's time I moved on with my life.

"Hey, big guy," says Owen. He usually stops by my cubicle on his way to the cafeteria. "You look over those specs I emailed you?" He's jumping lightly from one foot to the other, like a boxer, throwing fake punches at me. I don't fake-box back, in case I accidentally clip him with my sharp barnacled fist. I'm always very careful about things like that.

"Sure did," I tell him. "I was about to write you back."

"I'll look for your reply after lunch," Owen says.

He throws another right jab in the air, grins, and hops on down the hall. I've just had a thought. Instead of emailing him, I should join Owen for lunch and talk about my ideas face-to-face. I lean out my cubicle to see if he's still in sight. He's bouncing down the hall, popping his face into this workspace and that, so jocular and self-confident in his smooth human skin. I've never actually been to the cafeteria, though I've worked here for two years. So many people there I hardly know, so many prying eyes. I always pack a sack lunch and eat it at my desk. I peer out again. Owen is at the far end of the hall. He high-fives another coworker.

I settle into my chair, sighing, and pull up his email.

In the grocery store after work, a couple of teenaged girls are staring at me. I can tell they're daring each other to approach me. Finally one of them does. She's got spiky hair and her eyes are rimmed with eyeliner.

"Um, so, my friend wants to know?" she says. "What is that, like, all over your skin?"

"Barnacles," I tell her.

She looks at me like she's never heard of barnacles.

"Hard-shelled marine crustaceans," I explain—I know this drill so well—"that attached themselves to my surfaces."

"Ew," she says. Her lips have parted in surprise, and she leaves her mouth open like that, in a little seashell shape. "Um, why?"

Patient as can be, I tell her, "I used to be submerged in the sea," but she just keeps looking at me, mouth agape, as if that explains nothing.

Under the ocean, no one ever questioned my appearance. The whales didn't think there was anything funny-looking about me. The rocks never mocked me or crossed the street when they saw me coming. We all had barnacles. Under the ocean, I was ordinary.

"Can't you, like, get rid of them?"

This assumption that the barnacles are undesirable, that they're by definition ugly, is so hurtful I can't even tell you. "Why would I want to?" I say, challenging her, my voice shifting from patient to defiant.

"Uh, okay," the teenager says, eyeing her friend, who has been watching us from the shampoo aisle. "Never mind." She backs away and runs to her friend, and off they go, clutching each other and laughing.

I have to say I was hoping this kind of thing wouldn't happen in a small town. I thought everyone would get to know and accept me. But Stevens' Ferry isn't exactly a hamlet; it's a town-town, and it's a tourist attraction, too, so there are always strangers passing through.

"I waver," I later tell Alf, my therapist, "between anger and deep shame."

"Tell me about your anger," Alf says.

I shift in the plastic chair. It's not very comfortable, but when I started therapy I offered not to use Alf's good sofa, because I tend to snag upholstery. "I'm sick of being misunderstood. And I'm sick of the mocking. I shouldn't have to go through that."

"No, you shouldn't," Alf says gently. "But you aren't going to be able to stop people from behaving the way they do. The only behaviour you can change is your own."

"But I'm not doing anything wrong."

"It's not a question of right and wrong," he says. "Do you think it's possible that your reaction to people sometimes doesn't serve your own best interests?"

"What do you mean?"

"You've told me that you avoid people because you don't want them to make fun of you. You've also told me that you wish you had close friends, that you want someone to know you deeply. You can't have it both ways."

This work is too hard. I slump in the plastic chair. "Sometimes I think I deserve what I get. Because of what I've done."

"Oh, Gerald," Alf says, and delivers a little speech about the inevitability of error in this life and about the nevertheless inherent lovability of all creatures. Well, you can't put grief on a timetable. And sometimes I think Alf doesn't really understand remorse. He can't make grief and remorse go away with little speeches.

The gossip in the office is that Owen is dating Julia, the new accountant. They stop by my cubicle, holding hands, to say good-bye before leaving work for the day. They're going out to eat, they tell me, and then to the opening night of a production of Guys and Dolls.

"I'm happy for you," I tell Owen, when Julia goes back to her desk for a forgotten scarf. "You two make a cute couple." But privately I think this is going to effectively end my friendship with Owen, such as it is, because Julia is so uncomfortable around me. Owen is the closest thing I have to a buddy in the company. The closest thing I have to a friend in Stevens' Ferry, to be honest. He was my best shot at the kind of emotional life that Alf is trying to push me towards. Julia could get to know me a little, and look past the barnacles to the fellow underneath them, but I don't think she's going to.

I work late tonight. Not because I have so much work to do, but because I can hardly bear to go home to the quiet and the emptiness.

When I've had enough, I decide to walk home. It's far. Past the sleek, sterile edifices of the industrial park, one after another, and down a long unscenic stretch of road with no sidewalks, because no one was ever meant to walk here. Then cresting a hill and seeing the town itself below, lights arrayed in the foggy semi-dark.

Approaching downtown, I come upon the Community Arts Centre. In the window is a big poster advertising the 28th Annual Stevens' Ferry Poetry Slam, to take place next month right here. A poetry slam. That gives me pause for thought.

Then it starts raining. I don't have a raincoat or an umbrella with me, and it's bad to get wet. When my barnacles get wet they send up an overwhelming stench of seawater and decomposition. I'm standing under the awning of the café, trying to decide which is the quickest route home, when Owen and Julia push open the door of the Arts Centre and emerge onto the sidewalk. Ah, God. Owen sees me right away and hails me. "Hey!" he calls. "We're just coming from Guys and Dolls."

They're approaching fast, and I stink.

"We were thinking of getting some coffee. You wanna join us?"

"Actually, I'm in a bit of hurry. I'll see you at work tomorrow, and you can tell me all about it." I wave limply—hoping my arm movement doesn't send up a cloud of briny B.O.—and hurry away.

The impact of the stench on my social life is bad enough, but what's even harder for me is everything that it implies. The smell of wet barnacles is the smell of everything I've done wrong these last two years, the smell of betrayal, of mistakes made that can never be unmade, of suffering that is both deserved and unendurable. I start to run. The rain comes down heavily now, in cold sheets like waterfalls, and I'm running without looking where I'm going. I've stopped thinking about the shortest route to my apartment, and move blindly through wet streets. I leave the city centre, veering away from the lights and into a darker, sadder part of town. Past a bowling alley, a pawn shop. A bar that supposedly caters to gay werewolves. An adult bookstore. A disco. I'm just running, running, until my lungs are going to give out. I stop and put my hands on my knees, gasping for breath, and now I'm crying, my tears and the rain running together into the salty crevices between the barnacles on my skin, my tears running down into the barnacles, the rain pouring down into my eyes, all this salt and water threatening to drown me, as though I could be such a thing as drowned.

"Have you written about it?" Alf asks me in his gentle prodding way the next time we meet.

"About getting caught in the rain?"

"No, about your pain. About loss, and grief, and guilt. It might help you move through some of your feelings."

I don't say anything. I called in sick the day after the rain, staying home to dry out. Spent the day pressing various parts of myself to a space heater. I'm still a little damp—now and again I feel a dribble spill from a barnacle and run down my leg—but I don't smell any more. I'm okay.

"You mean, like, poetry?" Alf knows I write.

"Poetry. Journaling. Perhaps an essay."

I shake my head. But I'm thinking about it.

I take to walking home at night, early or late. I like the scruffy neighbourhoods, and I'm not worried about getting jumped; just the sight of me scares most people off. Besides, if someone tried to hurt me, he'd end up with some nasty scrapes. Some nights I would almost welcome the affront. Somebody comes after me? Thinks I'm a freak, alone and vulnerable? Thinks he'll have a little fun, roughing me up? Bring it on. I'll show 'em what Barnacle Man can do.

But no one ever does. Once I leave the werewolf bars and the peep shows behind, I am soothed by the sight of Stevens' Ferry laid out along the river with its city lights twinkling in the dusk. I especially enjoy my trips past the Community Arts Centre. The marquee, the posters of singers and actors, the excited hum of the crowds that linger in the lobby, all remind me that there was a reason I chose to live on land.

Then one day in therapy I mention my downtown walks and the musical that's playing, and Alf says, "Guys and Dolls—my wife and I are going to see it tonight!"

"I've never been to a musical," I tell him. "May I join you?"

Alf looks awkward for the slightest instant, then shifts into his compassionate, sensible therapist mode. "I can't spend time with clients socially, Gerald." He leans forward slightly. "It might endanger the client-therapist relationship."

"Oh."

"You understand, it would be the same for any client." I know what's going through his mind. He thinks I think he doesn't want to be seen with me in public because I'm covered with barnacles.

"I understand."

I realize now: Alf, not Owen, is the closest thing I have to a friend in Stevens' Ferry. The closest thing I have to a friend is my therapist. Who just made it very clear that he is not my friend. That is just pathetic.

I go home and sit down among my puzzles and books and CDs of whalesong; I pick up a pen. And it all pours out in anguished poems: how rotten I am, and how alone; how I can't get over my own errors in judgment, and how I don't deserve to because, after all, the barnacles will never get over it. How stupid I was to leave the sea, how naïve, how selfish, how I can never undo what is done. How I must martyr myself to the barnacles forever, because it is the closest I can come to making amends to them. How achingly alone it is to live on land, friendless, peerless, how I have exiled myself. Pages of verse gush out of me in cold sheets, a torrential downpour of rain and pain and tears: I cry an ocean and write an ocean of poems until it is all out of me.

The Annual Poetry Slam is a huge event in Stevens' Ferry. Everyone is there, everyone I know and hundreds of people I don't. I think there's a werewolf couple in the front row, two really hairy guys with big mutton-chop sideburns sitting kind of close together and listening intently to the readings. Of course you can't really tell from looking. That they're werewolves, I mean. But I think I recognize them from the bar I've walked past so many nights. Evidently the mayor is here, too, Mayor Esperanza Bajolaluna.

A woman with a cat on her shoulder reads a sonnet, and a funny little guy with a red wool hat recites some haiku in Norwegian, and then it's my turn. I step up to the podium. In the crowd are many of my coworkers. I spy Owen and Julia, holding hands again, near the front.

It gets very quiet as I read. People are listening hard, somber, intent. I've been quite prolific these past weeks, and have a lot of pieces to choose from. I chose carefully. Sometimes my audience members look surprised at what I have to say, and, as I finish the last poem, they are visibly moved. Then one of the wolfish guys up front stands and starts clapping his big hairy hands together, and someone off to the left stands, too, and pretty soon the whole café is pounding with applause.

There are a few readers after me, but none gets that kind of response. After the last poet slams, Mayor Bajolaluna takes the floor. She is a stout, dignified woman in a tweed suit. She makes a speech about how wonderful we all are, and how talented a place Stevens' Ferry is, and how proud it makes her. And then she says it's time to grant the award, and she turns my way and beams. "Gerald," she says, "I am pleased to award you this trophy for one of the most memorable poetry readings in the history of this contest, and to name you Poet Laureate of Stevens' Ferry for the coming year."

Afterwards Owen and Julia come to congratulate me, careful, of course, not to shake my hand.

"That was spectacular," Julia tells me. "I didn't even know you wrote poetry. And your work is so personal. I feel like I know you so much better now."

"This calls for a celebration," Owen says. "I'm going to order us some champagne." That's quite a nice gesture. Maybe Owen does think of himself as my friend.

Wednesday nights have been my therapy nights for nearly two years. But, as I tell Alf at my next session, I think I'm ready to use that time for something else now, something social. Owen and Julia and I have been hanging out some. We've made plans to attend the final recital of a local summer youth dance camp. I found out that Julia plays a mean game of Scrabble, too, so sometimes we play Scrabble on our lunch hour. I've joined a committee to help plan the company picnic that will take place next month. And Wednesday nights, I'm going to start attending poetry workshops at the Community Arts Centre.

"It's interesting," Julia says to me one afternoon in the cafeteria, "that you didn't read any poetry about your—skin."

I made a deliberate decision before the Poetry Slam not to share poems about grief or loneliness, about the sea, the barnacles, my identity as

Stevens' Ferry's lone Barnacle Man. I read poems I'd written about other aspects of my identity, aspects that have never crossed the minds of those who only see me as a big crusty rock on two legs. I wanted the poetry readers of Stevens' Ferry to understand me as a whole person: not to pretend to not see my barnacles, because the barnacles are part of who I am—but not reduce me to them, either.

"Why should I write only about my 'skin'?" I can hear the old prickliness in my voice.

"I'm sorry," Julia says right away. "I hope I haven't offended you. It's just that I imagine—it must be a big part of your life. But you hardly ever talk about it. I just always wonder about it. I'm—" She grasps for words, embarrassed.

Suddenly I see. "You're curious," I say.

"Yes."

Slowly, I hold out my arms for her. "I'm covered with barnacles," I tell her, turning my arms over so she can see both shell-bejewelled sides. "See? Hard-shelled marine crustaceans that attached themselves to my surfaces."

I expect her to look disbelieving or disgusted, but instead I see a look of relief in her pointy, perceptive little face; relief, maybe, that I'm willing to talk about it.

"I don't understand," she says. "How?"

"I used to live in the ocean. That's where I came from." People do always seem perplexed about this process of acquiring barnacles that seems so natural and obvious to me. I try to explain further. "I was never meant to be on land."

Usually my conversations about barnacles end at this juncture. But Julia looks long at my crustaceans, long but softly. "How did you end up in Stevens' Ferry?" she asks me.

"I wanted adventure," I tell her. "I wanted to try something new. And I got

it, all right. Everything in my life changed. Everything. Living here is like—
living someone else's life."

"How is it for you, living here? Are you sorry you left?"

I have to think before I tell her. "This is no place for barnacles. But once I'd
left, I didn't feel I ever could go home again. I didn't think they'd want me
back in the ocean, after I turned my back on it. I was homesick for a long
time. But now I think…" I look around me at the cafeteria, this place of dry
land and air, of smooth-skinned people, so alien, yet who have made room
for me. The company has provided me everything from professional development opportunities to barnacle-friendly office furniture. The city has provided me poetry and dance, and now recognition, too. And Stevens' Ferry
has given me people who will be my friends, if I let them. "Now I think
maybe this is home," I tell Julia.

She is still looking over the outcroppings of shells on my arms, on my neck
and face. "Are they uncomfortable?" she asks me.

I shake my head. The barnacles have never been uncomfortable. "They do
break sometimes," I tell her. "Once, when I was learning to walk on land,
I went down on one knee, hard, and all the shells on my knee shattered
and broke off." Now my knee is encrusted with just the bottom rims of
barnacles. I don't know if they could be scraped or pried off. But even if
they could be, I wouldn't do it. It would seem disrespectful. Like I wanted to rid myself of their vestiges. "I've had to make some adjustments. But
lately I've been thinking I'd like to stick around. I'm making a life for
myself here."

"And the barnacles?"

"The barnacles stay with me."

I will carry their tiny bodies always. Because it's my fault that they died. I
came out of the sea, and they couldn't survive in the air, the relentless air
without the caress of the tides, and they died. They all died, my nice barnacles. I wouldn't be able to bring them back to life, even if I returned to
the ocean. So I wear their shells in honour of their memory.

"You can touch one if you want," I tell Julia. "On the side. Look, it doesn't hurt. Just don't run your finger across the top, because they're sharp on top. Go on," I say. And she does.

Part 8

Short of Breath

I must have been sleeping, because I don't immediately recognize where I am or how long I've been here. Just that I'm lying in the dark. Trying to remember. It's very dark here, and stuffy. Hard to breathe. I do recall now: I've been sick. I'm in bed, sick. Actually, I'm feeling very much better. It must have been a good long, restorative sleep. I am quite stiff though. I must have been very deeply asleep and not moving much.

I say, the air is close here. Have to see if I can get a servant to come open a window. It must be the dead of night, it's so dark.

My gods, but my arms are stiff. I wonder if this is a manifestation of the fever I've had. I want to reach out and ring my little bell, but I find I can hardly lift a finger. It's starting to make me nervous. I wiggle my fingers, my hands. It's as though they're bound. By gods, they are bound. Not bound, now that I wiggle a bit more, but bandaged. Am I wounded? I don't recall. With a few minutes of effort I am able to lift my right arm. I run my hand over my left arm, my chest. Dear gods. Dear gods. I am entirely wrapped in cloth. Then it comes to me all at once what has happened and where I am.

It's not that I mind being dead—I know that great things await me—but what they didn't understand is that I can't stand being in closed spaces. I extend my hands out to either side and touch wood. Lift one hand and tentatively feel above me, to confirm my worst fear. It's true. I lie in a coffin.

Suddenly my heart is racing and I can't breathe. I am gasping for air, audibly, now crying out, now thrashing from side to side, weeping. How can they have done this to me? Someone must let me out.

Remember what Nanny taught me, when I had my attacks in the throne room, which was small and windowless. Take long, deep breaths. Count. Count. I can't, I can't do it. I thrash around until I'm exhausted. With fatigue the terror subsides just a little. I should summon Nanny's voice in my mind.

Count. Count. Take deep breaths. That's it. Until I am breathing normally again, and I can think.

All right then, the thing to do is pound out a distress signal until someone hears and comes and gets me. Unless I'm deep in the tomb already, in which case no one will ever hear me. Dear gods. I must put that thought out of my head. I put my fists up to the lid and bang one time. And the lid shifts. It shifts. It's not latched shut.

Relief floods my whole body. I push up again, and this time lift the lid a little so that a weak light seeps in. A beacon of hope. I push harder, am able to shove the lid off to one side and sit up. And then, albeit in a stiff and creaky fashion, to climb out of there.

I'm in the tomb, all right. It's high-ceilinged, spacious—thank gods, so I can breathe again—and lined with sarcophagi. It must not have been very long since they buried me, since torches are still burning. Some semblance of torches, anyway, giving off a faint but steady light there on the wall.

I take some time to look over my own sarcophagus. Separated, for some reason, from my coffins. It is very fine, as befits my station. Ornate, tasteful. I inspect the craftsmanship and find it to my liking. The artwork is of the highest quality, and the spells, in hieroglyphics around the base of the coffin, are accurate. I am pleased.

Who these other riffraff are here in the tomb with me, though, is another matter. Their coffins represent an aesthetic hodgepodge of styles. I don't recognize any of their names. It occurs to me that perhaps I have been dead a long time, and these fellows were buried after me. I can't quite wrap my mind around the concept.

Now what? I don't relish the idea of spending eternity in here, even if there is breathing room. I need to be outdoors. I need fresh air and sunshine, I need to feel the wind on my face and turn my gaze to the bracing blue sky. Nanny always let me be outside, except when I was required to be in the temple.

The sarcophagi rest behind red velvet ropes—an elegant touch, I must say—

and I have to step over them. I am terribly stiff. I do some toe-touches, some arm circles. Bits of dried resin crumble from my bandages as I move about.

The room where my coffin lies has a great wide opening that seems to lead to an even greater space. Thank gods. Just to move freely is a relief. I will see where this leads.

It leads to more rooms, and more rooms. They are full not of coffins but of works of art. My pride balloons. I have been given a finer burial than I ever imagined. I must have been truly revered by my people, to have been placed in such a vast tomb, and one so elaborately decorated. I can only imagine how many slaves it must have taken to build this edifice, and what it cost. They must have spared no expense to honour my memory, and send me to the after-life with enough art to stimulate my mind for all eternity, so great and beloved a leader was I.

I declare, I don't think much of some of this art. Room after room, and some of it taxes my patience. Like these big squares of colour. What is this supposed to be? Maybe they just put all their rejected art in here. They filled the place up so they could say they were giving me a good send-off. But really, they were cutting corners at my expense. Maybe, maybe, this is even a dishonour! Maybe they deliberately put bad art in here to punish me!

Now I'm so put out that I'm having a hard time breathing again. I sit down on a nearby chair. I've got to find some way of letting my displeasure be known. Since I'm conscious, and ambulatory, I imagine I can find a way out of here. I can go back to the city and give them a piece of my mind.

In truth, I didn't imagine the underworld to be like this. I thought there would be a clear passage to the other side. I didn't envision being stuck in here for-ever. And where are all the other dead kings? Why aren't they wandering around? There must be a way out. You'd think they would station some kind of guide here for us.

It occurs to me that they must have placed objects near my coffin for my use in death. I should go back and get them; they could come in handy.

Now, however, I'm not sure where I am. I've crossed through the room of square colours. On the other side is a room of irritating stone sculptures. Not just irritating, but sacrilegious, sculptures not of kings or gods but of unidentifiable shapes. I am more and more convinced that they did this on purpose to mock me. I wish I could remove these bandages. I'm flushed with irritation, and it's itchy and hot underneath the linen.

Beyond the heathenish sculptures is an empty hall. And posted there, looking patient and dignified, is a man in strange clothing. My guide! It must be him. I approach him and begin to explain. I wish to be taken at once to the afterlife, and when we get there he must arrange for these bandages to be removed and for refreshment to be brought. And I want to have a word with those in charge about the inappropriate decoration of this tomb. No, I want to do that first: register my displeasure, and then rest easy in the world to come. No: I've changed my mind. I want to get these wretched bandages off immediately, and I want a bath. I'm speaking to the guide in plain Demotic, but he's staring at me as though struck by lightning. "What's the matter with you?" I demand. "Are you simple?"

He stumbles backward and then turns and flees.

I am left alone in the empty marble hall. His footsteps echo away, and then nothing. The silence of the tomb.

How many hours have passed, I don't know. I wish to gods I were still asleep, asleep and oblivious in my coffin. I have wandered the whole of the tomb, every room of it, except the depths. There are stairs that lead down, and I do not wish to go there. I believe that way leads to the underworld. And I do not believe that I will pass the tests found there.

I am convinced now that the whole of this tomb is a vast, elaborate joke on me; my kingdom has dedicated a monument to my absurdity. It's a punishment for my hubris in life; I know it is. I bow my head in recognition of my former selfishness. And I accept the consequences. That my own people remember me not as a noble leader but as a demanding, self-absorbed young man, a greedy young man, a snob—this I recognize. And my punishment is fitting. I deserve just what they have given me. Should I venture into the underworld and attempt to cross to the afterlife, I will be deemed untrue of heart, unworthy of deed, and be gnawed by crocodiles, by snakes, by beetles.

Because of my late pride, I am condemned to this place between life and death. But the loneliness is getting to be too much to bear. The loneliness, and the bindings, which do not make me feel safe and held, but rather suffocated. They itch, they squeeze; I can't draw breath. Gods forgive me. What can I do to make amends? Is it too late? Am I damned forever?

The guide has not returned. Accustomed as I am to being surrounded by company—my advisors, my servants, my nanny—this solitude is deafening. There is no noise in here at all.

Except for the faintest whine, somewhere far away. A whine, and then a rough sound now and again, vaguely familiar. I think it's in the tomb somewhere. It must be. I move in the direction of the sound. I hear scratching, too, as of someone clawing or digging. Is there another like me here? Perhaps trying to leave his coffin? I press my ear to the wall. The sound seems to be coming from the other side, but there is no way to get there.

Unless through the underworld. It is the one passage I have not explored. Perhaps I am wrong about my unworthiness. Perhaps there is still time to be valiant, and the way down will lead to a way out. Or at least to a fellow traveller.

I have nothing left to lose. So I enter the stairwell. And go down. Ever so slowly and cautiously, because I am fearful now, and the panic is beginning to close in on my lungs again. I have to stop on the landing and breathe, count, count. But the whining and scratching grows louder. I do believe I am within reach of him, whoever he is. At the bottom of the stairs, an empty passage. No sign of snakes or beetles. Locked rooms. Another set of stairs, this time going up, and, at the top of it, loud sounds. I go up now, hopeful. At the head of these stairs, a door. And from the other side of the door, whining, and the rough sound I now recognize as a dog's bark.

I'm more of a cat person myself, but I'm so lonely, I'd welcome anyone's company. I open the door and a great hulking pointy-faced dog with big black ears, looking something like the dog-headed god Anubis, stands on his hind legs and licks my face.

It all makes sense to me now. Anubis is the god of embalming and of the dead.

Obviously, this dog—not that simpleton in the funny clothes—is my guide to the afterlife.

There doesn't seem to be anywhere to go. We're in a dark and empty passage. I'm so happy to have company, I don't care for a long time about being dead and trapped. But after a few hours my bandages get my attention again. By gods, they itch. I have an idea. I think I'm just going to unwrap myself. I don't need a servant to do it! I will try doing something for myself, for once.

I'll start at the feet, I guess. They're bound up pretty tight, but my fingernails have grown since I expired, and I'm able to slide a nail under the bottommost bandage and pull it away. It's a slow, dusty job, tugging this way and that, but I manage to free my whole foot.

Here's the hard part: my foot is unsightly. In life I had the feet of a nobleman, slender, brown, shapely as befitted my station. My nanny used to wash my feet and praise them.

My smooth brown skin is all gone. The flesh of my foot is dried like crocodile meat; desiccated and wrinkled as tree bark, grey, horrible. The tendons and bones show through like the foot of a very, very old person. It's a blow. I hadn't thought before about how I'd look underneath my wrappings. I feel another panic coming on. But the bandages make me feel worse, more breathless, and I'm dying to get them off. Forget vanity. I yank on the loose end and pull. It's easier now that I've got a good start. A considerable length comes unravelled, all the way up to my thigh. My leg is beastly, grey, I can't look, but it feels wonderful to bare it to the open air.

I want to stand on it and see how it feels.

And the most horrifying thing happens. When I put weight on my newly freed leg, it just crumbles. It turns to dust, and falls like a shovelling of dirt to the ground. My leg, turned utterly to ash, a few stray shards of bone poking up through the pile.

Splendid. Now I'm one-legged. Anubis cocks his head and whimpers. He sniffs at the dust and at the dusty stump of my thigh. I guess I have been dead a very, very long time. So long that my body is only dust held together with tape.

So long that there may no longer be any memory of me. No memory of my life's trespasses and vices. Gods! Can you hear me? Isn't it time for me to be released?

A strange light is filling the space. Early morning light is pouring in from the end of the passage. The outdoors! We have found a way out!

I have to move one-legged as best I can, leaning against the wall of the passage, hopping. Twice I fall. Anubis licks my face. But it isn't all that far. It takes all my strength to open the door of glass at the blessed daylit end of this tomb's entrance. It is heavier than the lid to my sarcophagus. But I do it, and pitch forward onto grassy green earth. The smell of plants, of the open air, is heaven. I can't believe it. I am profoundly grateful.

Anubis is grateful too, bounding, barking. "Please don't abandon me," I tell him, and he doesn't. But he's got a playful gleam in his eye. He grabs the loose end of my leg bandage in his toothy mouth and starts to pull.

"No!" I cry. If he unravels me, I'll turn all to dust; I'll have no body. He pulls, and I start to come undone. He gives a naughty bark, and pulls and pulls, rolling me over a few times. I'm breaking up inside my bandages, going to pieces even before he's got the wrappings off. Anubis is on a tear now, bounding back and forth with my cloth, increasingly floppy, in his mouth, shaking his head, tossing me in the air and catching me in that great maw, pawing at me and snuffling, shoving his great snout into the dust that was once my noble body. I'm all unwrapped now, a heap in the grass, scattered, earth like the earth I lie on. Anubis trots away. My sense of betrayal and despair is so great I am unable to fathom it.

And then a thing happens. My spirit lifts, gathers itself up out of the dust and rises, and I float up on a current that carries me above my tomb. Anubis is below me, trotting in the grass, and I realize that he has liberated me. I owe him a deep debt of gratitude. I will never be able to repay him, though, because I am floating higher now, above the trees, the dust of my body no longer visible. I see that my tomb lies alongside the water, alongside a stretch of the Nile that is unknown to me, though pretty, with a lovely spread of trees and artful structures nearby. I understand that I was wrong about the art, about the

79

mocking. I don't know why my tomb was done up the way it was, but I know I was not dishonoured, though I perhaps deserved to be. But it is all past; it is all dust. Contrition and time have dissolved everything. I have been freed, and I can breathe now at last, deeply, I am unbound, I float up into the bracing blue.

About the Author

Jan Underwood was born in Pennsylvania, has lived in Canada, Mexico and France and now makes her home with her daughter in Portland, Oregon. She teaches Spanish at a community college and writes, acts and plays the piano in her spare time. *Day Shift Werewolf* is her first novel.

About the contest

The 3-Day Novel Contest is a put-your-keyboard-where-your-mouth-is rite of passage for anyone who has ever said "I'm going to write a novel some day." The contest started in 1977, when a handful of restless Vancouver writers accepted a dare to write an entire novel in a single long weekend. They did it again the following year and a tradition was born. Today, hundreds of writers from all over the world step up to this challenge every Labour Day Weekend, all vying for the grand prize of publication. The published winners, together with thousands of creative first drafts, are a unique contribution to world literature and have become their own literary genre.

The International 3-Day Novel Contest is now an independent organization but it owes its existence to the past efforts of Arsenal Pulp Press, Anvil Press and Blue Lake Books. We at the 3-Day Novel Contest and 3-Day Books thank these publishers and *Geist* magazine, along with the many judges, volunteers and friendly cultural organizations who offer their time and support to keep this tradition going.

For information on other past winning 3-Day Novels and details on how to enter the contest, please visit www.3daynovel.com.

Previous Winners of the International 3-Day Novel Contest

Order these and other 3-Day Novels from www.3daynovel.com, or ask for them at your local bookstore.

Love Block

Meghan Austin and Shannon Mullally

Through a series of correspondences, two secret agents debate, bicker and commiserate while they search for a mysterious cure for the lovelorn. *Love Block* was written via phone and email by two writers living on opposite ends of the United States. It's funny, furious, sometimes crazy and always fast-moving, just like the contest itself.

ISBN 1-55152-194-6

"...the whole project goes beyond language, i.e., beyond the normal and expected scope of a novel. Even the act of reading it is participation in the project and in the game."
—Bookslut.com

Struck

Geoffrey Bromhead

Meet Finnigan Heller, drifter: reclusive, abrasive and clairvoyant. He's also been struck by lightning more times than you've had hot dinners. Heller's bizzare gift has him on the run from a scientist, an intelligence agent, and an Englishman with a taste for violence. *Struck* is a story about thunderstorms, Heisenberg's Uncertainty Principle, the nature of luck and the fate of one very attractive nose. ISBN 1-895636-53-1

Socket

David Zimmerman

Ronald Percy, an international aid worker, travels to Ethiopia to assist with an irrigation project for the African Development Organization. Upon arrival, he is unable to locate his agents or company representatives, and soon finds himself enmeshed in a web of bureaucracy and state corruption. ISBN 1-895636-42-6

Body Speaking Words

Loree Harrell

A novel about—what else—writing a novel in the space of three days. Harrell offers insights into family, friendship, growing up female. *Body Speaking Words* is a poignant, funny and sexy account of one woman's attempt to understand what drives us to document the essential stories of our lives. ISBN 1-895636-09-4

Skin

Bonnie Bowman

Salacious, funny, and painfully emotive, *Skin* is a provocative and ruminative parable about our deep-rooted urge to ostracize the freakish and shun the disfigured among us.

In this unconventional love story, Bowman probes the surface to reveal deeper, more lingering impulses connected to desire, understanding, and love. A cutting and startling debut novel. *Skin* won the Re-Lit Award in 2001. ISBN 1-895636-32-9

Small Apartments

Chris Millis

A capricious comedy of errors, *Small Apartments* resonates with tremulous energy and memorable characters. Franklin Franklin is a fully realized and sympathetic protagonist in the vein of Ignatius Reilly (*A Confederacy of Dunces*), a simple man who yearns for "a land of pastoral serenity" devoid of the irritants of contemporary urban society. An off-beat tale, *Small Apartments* is accented along the way by murder, strange fingernail collections and the occasional blast from a treasured alphorn. ISBN 1-895636-35-3

The Underwood

P.G. Tarr

Holden Caufield meets Barton Fink. A hotel with a past, a place that has failed to maintain the pace of present day life and now languishes in disrepair ... Enter Foster Lutz, a twenty-one-year-old pianist who lands the job of lounge entertainer in this once elegant establishment and *The Underwood*—including the lives of its inhabitants—is set for a spell of splendour and rejuvenation. ISBN 1-895636-17-5

Wastefall

Stephen E. Miller

Forrest thinks the world is a garbage dump, a surreal wasteland in which anything can happen. A series of circumstances forces him to abandon reality and search for fulfillment amidst the debris of a disposable society. Sold as a screenplay to Crescent Entertainment. Stephen Miller has since published *The Woman in the Yard* and *The Field of Mars*.

ISBN 0-88978-220-2

Shades (aka Dr. Tin)

Tom Walmsley

The first winner of the 3-Day Novel Contest tells a gritty tale about a mass murderer, a musician, a dominatrix and a private eye. Some of them will die. Some have died before. Tom Walmsley has since penned several plays and screenplays, including the controversial films "Paris, France" and "Blood." ISBN: 0-88978-254-7

Tacones

Todd Klinck

This rollicking and caustic expose of the violent and ambivalent nature of the Toronto "after-hours" scene and its inhabitants became an instant underground hit.

ISBN 1-895636-14-0

Still

b.p. nichol

A haunting novel from one of Canada's most distinguished avant-garde poets. A work of profound emotional depth, subtlety and intensity. ISBN 0-88978-146-X

Stolen Voices/Vacant Rooms

Steve Lundin and Mitch Parry

The first and only shared prize of publication. One, a nightmarish vision of a land in decline; the other, a finely crafted piece of prose, rich in mood and evocative in its language. ISBN 1-895636-06-X

Accordion Lessons

Ray Serwylo

The story of a Ukrainian family in post-war Winnipeg, *Accordion Lessons* is sad, funny, eloquent and both full of tenderness for things lost and enthusiastic about what can be found. ISBN 0-88978-122-2

Nothing So Natural

Jim Curry

A twelve-year-old boy longs for ordinary existence amid extraordinary circumstances. *The World According to Garp* written from the other side of the tracks. ISBN 0-88978-167-2

This Guest of Summer

Jeff Doran

He's a high-tech millionaire-in-progress, she's a ballerina. Their love is as fragile as his ambitions and her bones. ISBN 0-88978-151-6

Circle of Birds

Hayden Trenholm

An impressionistic, finely-wrought tale of lost memory, tangled history, despair and discovery. ISBN 1-895636-03-5

"An unsettling meditation on the passage of time and the nature of identity."

—*Books in Canada*

Ruby Ruby

Bradley Harris

Ruby Ruby is a soft-boiled murder mystery that follows the trail of an expatriate Canuck as he tries to sleuth out the answers to a puzzling series of pointless and apparently motiveless murders: Who'd want to kill a sixtyish night watchman guarding an abandoned pie factory? ISBN 1-895636-23-X